# Conall

## THE K9 FILES

# Dale Mayer

CONALL: THE K9 FILES, BOOK 24
Beverly Dale Mayer
Valley Publishing Ltd.



ISBN-13: 978-1-778863-02-8
Print Edition

# Books in This Series

Ethan, Book 1
Pierce, Book 2
Zane, Book 3
Blaze, Book 4
Lucas, Book 5
Parker, Book 6
Carter, Book 7
Weston, Book 8
Greyson, Book 9
Rowan, Book 10
Caleb, Book 11
Kurt, Book 12
Tucker, Book 13
Harley, Book 14
Kyron, Book 15
Jenner, Book 16
Rhys, Book 17
Landon, Book 18
Harper, Book 19
Kascius, Book 20
Declan, Book 21
Bauer, Book 22
Delta, Book 23
Conall, Book 24
Baron, Book 25
Walton, Book 26

Boxed Sets and Bundles
https://geni.us/Bundlepage

# About This Book

Welcome to the all new K9 Files series reconnecting readers with the unforgettable men from SEALs of Steel in a new series of action packed, page turning romantic suspense that fans have come to expect from USA TODAY Bestselling author Dale Mayer. Pssst… you'll meet other favorite characters from SEALs of Honor and Heroes for Hire too!

Conall is more than happy to head out after a War Dog has gone missing, leaving a wheelchair-bound military war veteran lost and alone. Yet what seems like a simple job takes an unsavory turn, when Conall comes face-to-face with darker undertones in that town.

Bethany always wanted to have her own veterinary clinic, and she's been doing a decent job of it, until so much of the town died that she finds it hard to get and to keep decent staff. Her temporary help suddenly embroils her clinic in a mess involving a missing War Dog, and then Bethany uncovers what else this young lady is involved in. None of it's good.

Conall refuses to back down or to walk away from the sudden hell Bethany's life has become. No telling how ugly this can get …

**Sign up to be notified of all Dale's releases here!**
https://geni.us/DaleNews

# PROLOGUE

K AT GRINNED WHEN she opened the door to see Delta standing there with Rebecca. "Now, don't tell me," she greeted them. "You need an ankle joint."

Delta smiled broadly, genuinely happy to see her, and beginning to allow himself to feel the effects of the past several days.

Kat continued. "You may be surprised to hear that I have some parts for you." Then she looked over at Rebecca, smiled, and nodded. "Hi, it's nice to meet you. I'm Kat."

"Hi," Rebecca replied shyly.

Kat studied the pretty woman, who looked as if her life had been flipped upside down. Yet somehow she'd landed upright. "Rough couple days, *huh*?" she asked Rebecca.

"You're not kidding," she murmured. "Yet it seems that all good things end well."

"And that's what we count on." Kat nodded and smiled as she eyed Rebecca. "I also hear that you've done some work on prosthetics."

"Yes, but on animals though," she clarified. "So I don't know how helpful that would be to you."

"Are you kidding? It's already helpful, especially if you know your way around a wrench, a screwdriver, a hammer drill, and a few other tools."

"Yeah, I do," she said. "All very necessary on the electronic circuit board side of things."

"Good," Kat declared, with a huge smile. "Are you looking for a job or just looking to take a holiday?"

"Well, a holiday for a little bit would be nice," Rebecca replied, "and I still have to get some of my stuff moved out."

"We can just hire a company for that," Kat noted, with a wave of her hand. "There are people in the world who do that sort of thing. We've got other things to do." She heard her husband coming to join them and looked over at Badger, a big smile on her face.

Badger walked up, introduced himself to Rebecca, and smiled. "How you doing there, Delta?"

"I'm doing great," he stated, as he wrapped an arm around Rebecca's shoulders. "If I'd realized this is the kind of shit you guys were handling—"

"You would have run in the opposite direction," Badger stated.

Delta laughed. "I might have run, but only because I wouldn't have understood." He shook his head. "Now I understand, and that's a whole different story." He leaned over and kissed Rebecca hard on the cheek. "This would have made any trip perfect."

Badger chuckled, looked over at Kat, and teased, "So, I guess you got another successful matchmaking feather in your cap. What will you do now?"

"Yep, I did, and I already know who I have in mind for the next job. But first things first." She looked over at Rebecca and offered, "Why don't you come into the office tomorrow, and we'll see if it's a match."

Badger's gaze lit with interest. "You guys think you can work together?"

Rebecca smiled. "I'm game, if Kat's game. All I've heard

about is this ankle joint of Delta's."

That set Kat off into giggles again. Badger just shook his head. "I swear to God, these two? All they deal with is that ankle."

"But I was thinking blue steel would be cool, maybe with some filigree metal all through it," Rebecca suggested. "That would be awesome."

At that, Badger looked at her with interest.

Kat's gaze lit up, and she nodded. "I really would like to get more artistic with some of this. That would be amazing." And, with that, the two women headed off to have a chat.

Badger called out to his wife, and Kat turned and looked at him. He asked her, "What about the next one?"

"That's all right," she said. "I'll get there. I already have Conall tagged for it."

He stopped, his hands on his hips, and asked, "Why him, for crying out loud?"

She smiled. "Because he'd be perfect for this next one." And, with that, Kat turned and walked into the kitchen, her arm wrapped around Rebecca, as they talked about ankle joints.

Badger turned to face Delta, shaking his head. "Well?"

"Yeah, *well*," he replied, with a knowing smile. "Outside of an ankle joint, I could really use a beer."

Badger chuckled and slapped him on the shoulder. "Out to the pool then. That's where the beer and the relaxation happens," he declared. "That was a job well done, by the way. Now, if only Kat wasn't thinking about Conall for the next one."

"Why is that?"

"Because he's big, a little on the rougher-built side. Yet he's all heart and a big marshmallow. If it's a bad case, he's bound to go to pieces."

Delta frowned at him. "I think you're considering that from the wrong angle. If it goes bad, his heart will hurt, and then he'll move on, stronger and better than ever. But that marshmallow? We need guys like that. Most of the world is too scared and too ashamed to show any emotions. Guys like Conall, they're all emotion, but they're also really good men to have behind you."

Badger nodded. "Agreed. So Kat was right, … once again."

# CHAPTER 1

CONALL BURKE HAD a million questions, and they all remained unanswered. He drove toward the address Kat had given him, to deal with the case of missing War Dog Bacchus. Conall didn't have a clue what he would do about it, even if the dog were still missing. He understood from the other guys working with Badger on various projects that he and Kat had been locating lost War Dogs for the last year or so, and they'd just received another four cases.

It didn't say much for the War Department that this many War Dogs would be missing, but since hundreds if not thousands or even tens of thousands of these dogs had been trained, maybe the ratio of lost dogs wasn't that bad. This case, well, it struck a little too close to home for Conall. This lost War Dog had been adopted by Michael Stanford, a retired veteran, who had lost a leg.

Conall wondered if his matching injury wasn't part of what was in the back of Kat's mind. She was a devious woman, presumably with the best of intentions, though it often didn't appear that way. He loved her dearly, but he just never quite understood her. No one knew where she was coming from, except maybe Badger. She always came from the heart, so Conall trusted her. Still, when she looked at you, something else was going on in those knowing eyes.

Conall shifted in the driver's seat of his old truck, grateful that he'd been asked to travel a little closer to home than the other guys had. With only one more state line to cross, he played the audio file of the interview on his phone as he drove. He understood a part of the problem was that Bacchus had been placed with an older veteran who was in a wheelchair. He still had some mobility, but the wheelchair was to help him get around a lot easier. The dog was part companion and part guard dog, and everything had been going fine—until the nephew had moved in to help out the old man. Then it wasn't long before the dog started disappearing throughout the day.

It started off as a little bit of straying. Then his absences went longer and longer. The uncle and nephew had no idea where Bacchus went, and any attempt to keep the dog locked up inevitably ended. As soon as Bacchus went out to do his business, he took off. He came back, but there was always a time lag. One of these times, whether coming or going, nobody seemed to know which, he was hit by a vehicle, taken to the veterinarian for treatment, then kept overnight.

According to Michael, when Bacchus was released the next day, somebody other than his nephew picked up the War Dog, and nobody seemed to know where Bacchus went from there.

A neighbor had asked him what had happened to the War Dog. She herself had applied to get one and had been refused, so she'd been keeping an eye on this one and was always friendly with it. When Michael told her what had happened, she reported it to the War Department.

Somehow that had come back down to Badger and Kat. Conall shook his head at the way things filtered through in the military. He didn't have any reason to suspect Michael of anything bad going on, but the fact that the dog's behavior changed after the nephew arrived did raise alarms. The behavioral change in a dog didn't happen for no reason. Conall couldn't say for sure that Bacchus was being abused or in any way mistreated, particularly by the nephew, yet that's when the change had happened. Conall would definitely take a closer look at the nephew.

The other problem was the old man hadn't reported it and apparently hadn't found the missing dog. Now it had been weeks, so it would be all that much harder to track down where the dog had ended up. The vet clinic claimed that they received a note, saying that the dog should be released to the nephew, and it was signed by Michael, the primary caretaker. The old veteran stated that he hadn't signed any such thing, that it was just a complete fabrication, and that he wanted his dog back.

That was an interesting point because, should the note exist, it did release the animal hospital of any kind of liability, but they should have checked with the owner first regardless.

The War Dog had been going in for its regular shots and checkups, and it was not uncommon for somebody else to take the dog in, as the old man had transportation issues, given his wheelchair, and his car was not modified for that. The nephew stated that he knew nothing about the vet visit or about the War Dog being released.

Shutting off the recording, Conall noted his turnoff up ahead. It took another twenty minutes or so to reach the small town where the dog had been living. Then Conall pulled off on the roadside and checked his GPS to see exactly where he was going. He listened to the rest of the audio file, which noted that the dog had served as an IED-locator dog and had done some chemical warfare work as well. He had been injured in one of his last missions, losing one of his legs, and had to be retired.

The dog had recovered from his war injuries and was still healthy, with three limbs intact, but he was no longer suited for the type of work he used to do. He didn't handle loud noises well, which could also explain why he may have taken off. If a vehicle had backed-fired in the area around him or if he'd heard some sound that upset him, he may have just charged off.

If Bacchus had already detached from the old man and had become used to doing different things during the day with others or just solo, it's quite possible the War Dog wouldn't come home. Bond formation between dog and owner was critical, and here, the bond didn't appear to be strong enough to keep him grounded. If the dog didn't like the nephew for some reason, that would be more motivation to leave. It all depended on the strength of Bacchus's bond with the old veteran, if there even were one to begin with.

Conall had plenty of things to consider, but nothing terribly suspicious, just things he needed to question and to check out. He pulled into a small roadside gas station and café, filled up his tank, hoping to find a coffee and a sandwich or something before he stopped in at the old vet's home to talk to him. The old man should be expecting him, but that didn't mean he would be looking for him today. Most people thought that they'd get a phone call or something along that line, but Conall was much more of an in-person kind of guy.

Parking his truck in a back lot, after having filled it up with fuel, he headed inside the café and sat down at a table in the back corner. He preferred to have his back protected and to watch the door. Maybe it was to look for an easy exit;

he didn't know.

Conall's tours in the military seemed like a long time ago, yet remnants were still right here with him today in many ways. The PTSD would never go away, but he was managing it and would take that any day. His prosthetic leg with the knee joint was something that Kat was working on, and, so far, they'd done pretty well, and he was pleased with the progress he'd made. Was there more just waiting to be had? Absolutely. But that wasn't on Kat. She had done a phenomenal job and so had the surgeons.

It was easy to forget how far Conall had come in the last year. Still, he used to live another life, one that he loved and enjoyed, but everything was different now. Aside from this mission, he was currently looking after the family homestead, where he had a house to himself, in New Mexico, wondering what his life would be like from here on out. He'd been cleared to go back to work, whatever work that he chose, and he would be on military disability for the rest of his life. That did give him a certain amount of freedom, but it wasn't enough to give him full financial freedom.

So, some sort of vocation would be a good idea. He'd spent a fair amount of time working with Badger's crews, as they built houses to help other veterans, and Conall really enjoyed that kind of work. No pressure, a little money. It had kept him busy, which was good. He just didn't know what he wanted to do from now on. He could continue to do that and still do something else. He wasn't limited to just one side job.

He felt as if he needed to do something more, but the difference between a need and a want wasn't that easy to determine. In reality, he was just bored. This War Dog job—and he wasn't even sure it really was a job—was a change. No money was involved; it was all about helping an animal, and Conall certainly had used these animal skills to his advantage in the Middle East. So, if Badger and Kat needed help, Conall was certainly willing to do his part and to give back.

He was feeling a little edgy these days, and that was probably most of the problem he had being with Badger. Conall wondered if that was why Kat had chosen him for this job, but he didn't know for certain. He wouldn't worry about it now. He was here. He was okay to be here, and, if the War Dog needed him, Conall would do his best to find Bacchus and to help as much as he could. He adored animals of all kinds and honestly found them easier to be with than people, a good share of the time.

He'd heard rumors about Timber wanting to start a sanctuary. That was a hell of an idea, and Conall could see himself helping out with that, but so much mystery surrounded Timber. Thus Conall didn't know what was truth and what was rumor. Still, the guy was fascinating. Timber had a lot of stories, if you could get him to open up and talk. Most of the time, Timber didn't say anything. He just looked at you with that gaze that kind of slipped right into your soul.

"Wonder why they never ask him to do these War Dog jobs?" Conall murmured under his breath. Maybe they would, or maybe it was just part and parcel of all Kat's shenanigans. She seemed to have an uncanny idea of who could do what, like an all-seeing eye, and she chose the people for the job based on that. Hell, Conall didn't know. He just knew he should do this job, based on Kat's urging.

When he sat back with a hot cup of black coffee and a menu to peruse, he smiled as he looked around the small coffee shop. It brought to mind a million of these odd little cafés all around the country. Something was both welcoming and timeless about them, and, for him, it was almost a security. The familiarity allowed him to relax just a little bit more.

Conall considered asking the staff and the customers if they had seen Bacchus, providing them with the photo that Conall had on his phone. Yet something held him back from that. He didn't quite know his surroundings yet, so he thought he would test the waters first.

When a group of young men came in—loud, noisy, and rude—Conall felt himself tensing up. He knew guys like these. They were just the same as so many others all around the world, men who hadn't served their country and had no sense of loyalty because they had never really ever been tested.

They thought they knew what made everything work in life, but really, until you've had to prove your point or had to stand up for what you believe in, it was all talk. So, when it came to action, there were a lot of excuses from these bully types.

They sat down not too far from Conall and started hassling the waitress for coffee immediately. He shook his head, as she immediately came over and dropped menus on the table for them, with a coffeepot in hand. She was smiling and jovial, but Conall noted the wariness in her eyes. He watched the byplay with interest, wondering whether these were regulars and if she had to deal with this on an ongoing basis or if this group was here for the first time.

When one guy started to get snippy with her, she shook her head. "No, none of that. I'm not talking to you if you'll speak to me like that."

"If you don't give us that damn coffee like we asked for it," demanded this same guy, "you've got no business complaining. I asked for service, and you should be giving it to me."

She stared at him for a long moment. "Maybe I should call Old Joe out here, and you can tell him that."

"Yeah, maybe you should," he spat. "Shit, I don't even know why I keep coming here."

"I don't know either." She studied him with a wary eye.

Conall noted that she was probably in her mid-fifties or so and looked like she had seen this guy's type way too much. Conall watched carefully as the bully got a little more obnoxious.

Another of the men in his group added, "Calm down, Jake. We're just here for coffee. You don't have to go causing a headache wherever we go."

"I just want coffee too," he snapped, turning to glare at his friend. "Why the hell do you get coffee the way you want it, and I don't?"

"Maybe you need to change the way you ask for it," his buddy suggested, with a jeer.

Jake snorted, crossed his arms, and leaned on the table. He stared up at the waitress. "How about you just go get me what I asked for?"

"We don't have that here," she stated in an irate, yet still considerate tone. "You ask for it every time you're here, and the answer is always the same."

At that, Conall's gaze was caught by a movement behind the counter. An old man, his thick beefy arms the size of hams, stepped out and bellowed, "Is that you causing trouble again, Jake? You know better than to hassle my waitresses."

Jake turned and glared in his direction. "I am not hassling her. She's hassling me. And, just so you know, I just wanted a cup of coffee."

"No, you don't *just* want a cup of coffee," Joe clarified bitterly. "You want one of those fancy things that we don't offer. You also know very well that we don't offer it here, so why the hell are you still asking? Go down the street. Plenty other coffee shops will give it to you."

"I definitely would if I could, but these guys here? … They all want to come to this place." Jake shook his head. "I don't have a clue why."

"Doesn't matter either way. Now get lost. You don't need to be coming in here, causing trouble all the time. Go find some other place to hassle, if you're gonna act that way." And, with that, Old Joe stepped forward and out from behind the counter, glaring at him. "Don't make me get physical."

At that, Jake snorted. "Old man, you are way past the point of getting physical."

"Don't matter if I am or not," he stated, "because I would go down fighting, and you damn well know it, and then you will have that stench on your hand."

"I am not looking for trouble. I told you that."

Conall just watched with interest, as Old Joe tried to get Jake to take a walk, but Jake wasn't looking for any kind of appeasement. He was out looking for trouble and intent on finding it.

When the waitress came back in his direction, Conall quickly placed his order and watched as she returned to the other table. She asked if they wanted to place an order or if they just wanted coffee.

"You know I want coffee," Jake snorted, then got up, shoving the table back. "If I can't get it here, guess I'll get it somewhere else."

She just stepped out of the way, watching as he got up, either to leave or to cause more trouble. Jake stood by the door, obviously ready to leave.

Conall felt his own muscles tense, as he readied himself for a fight that wasn't even his.

The woman looked over at him and frowned immediately, almost a silent communication between the two of them. When she gave an ever-so-slight shake of her head, Conall relaxed, realizing that this was probably something that occurred on a regular basis. If they could solve it without violence, they would, but the waitress was really hoping not to have any more fights in her workplace.

Conall settled back and watched as Old Joe stayed out front the whole time that the bully was here. When his buddies finally finished their coffee, Jake looked over at the old man. "We ain't paying for this either."

Old Joe nodded. "Yeah, that's what you usually do. Come in here, cause trouble, and walk away without paying. I know all too well that's the only reason you come in here because you figure you can get it for free."

Jake snorted. "Why should I pay for the pathetic sludge you've got here?"

"Why drink it then?" he asked, looking at him with an intensity that confirmed how Old Joe had seen more in his lifetime than he cared to, and he knew exactly what this bully was all about.

"I sure as hell ain't paying." Jake turned to the rest of his crew. The two guys with him flushed and bolted immediately, but neither of them paid either.

Conall stared, then got up and walked to the door, as the waitress called out, "Are you not eating either?"

"Oh, I'm definitely eating," he replied, as he stepped out and quickly took a picture of Jake's license plate, just as the man stepped on the gas pedal, and the vehicle barreled out noisily. Walking back in, Conall sat back down at his table. The waitress looked at him, puzzled, as he shrugged. "With riffraff like that, I like to know who they are and what the hell they're up to."

Old Joe snorted. "They're up to the same shit they've always been up to. They think that they own the world and that the world should pay for them."

Just as he finished speaking, the door slammed open, and Jake walked back in. The waitress immediately stepped forward, "Now what?"

"That asshole," he yelled, pointing at Conall, "took a picture of our vehicle."

She frowned at him. "So what? Maybe he wants a truck like that for himself."

Jake glared at Conall, who just sipped his coffee, completely ignoring him. Jake hesitated, not sure what he should do, and then he snorted. "Better make sure that's all he was doing," And, with that, he stormed back out again.

Conall watched him leave. "Is he always like that?"

Old Joe nodded. "Yeah, the whole gang runs like that." He shook his head. "They come around every once in a while, acting like they're somebody special, somebody who doesn't have to play by anybody's rules, and they get to do whatever they want." He shrugged. "You can fight it all you want, but they would just bring the rest of their gang in here and cause even more trouble."

"Is that what this town is all about?" Conall asked, but he knew better than to expect an answer. "Doesn't sound too good to me."

Old Joe stared at him. "You're obviously a stranger."

"I am. I came into town to see an old man called Michael."

At that, his eyebrows popped up. "Now he's a friend of mine. What do you want with him?" he asked, his voice barely above outright suspicion.

"He lost a War Dog," Conall replied casually. "I'm here to try and find it." He showed them Bacchus's photo and asked if they had seen him in the last couple weeks. Both the waitress and Old Joe looked at him, stumped, shaking their heads. Conall nodded, understanding their hesitation to believe him. "Believe it or not, there are people out there who care when things like that happen."

"I sure as hell wish they cared about other stuff here too," Joe muttered, "like that riffraff you just saw walk out of here."

"Those guys," Conall asked, looking over at him, "live here?"

"Sure do," the waitress confirmed. "Years ago, when they were in high school, they weren't as bad, but they sure weren't good. They didn't give a crap about school, didn't give a crap about anything. It's not a surprise how they turned out."

"And, of course, they never served their country either, right?" Conall asked.

She shook her head. "Not too many people around here do."

"Do they give Michael a problem about that?"

"Sometimes," she said, with a nod. "People around here don't seem to have a whole lot of respect for veterans."

"I see," Conall replied. "That's interesting."

"If you're thinking about bucking against any of

them"—Old Joe snorted from behind the counter—"you better get yourself a shotgun because these guys? … They don't play nice."

"Have they ever done any serious damage here?" Conall asked. The more information he had, the better off he would be.

"No, they just come around looking for free coffee."

"Interesting, what about food?"

"Not often. They usually just insult the hell out of us, and then they take off, as if they want to push it, but don't. They probably would if they had a little more balls," Old Joe said, then laughed. "Yet it's to my advantage that they don't. I don't move as quickly as I used to, and this woman here, … Rosalind, she's hell on customers with a fry pan. She keeps it stashed behind the counter here, just for the sake of those unsavory characters, but it doesn't seem to matter. That riffraff has taken over the town."

Conall shook his head. "Sad times."

"Absolutely," Old Joe agreed with a murmur, "but just because it's a sad time doesn't mean anybody gives a shit about changing it."

"You know anything about the local animal clinic?"

"My daughter works there," Rosalind stated. "What's she got to do with anything?"

He frowned at her. "Who said she did? I'm not suggesting anybody had anything to do with the missing War Dog. I'm just asking where I can find the clinic. I want to talk to them because the War Dog was getting treated there, right before he disappeared. I just want to know what kind of shape and condition he was in around the time he disappeared."

"You're really here hunting a War Dog?" she asked, puzzled.

"Yeah, I'm *really* here hunting a War Dog," he repeated, with a nod. "They served our country, and they deserve our care."

She nodded. "I always wondered about that, whether anybody gave a damn," she muttered. "It seems like so much of the world's been left to forage it on its own, and nobody cares anymore. Like the liars and cheats abound, and nobody else gives a crap."

"I don't know about that," Conall countered. "We do get ugly pockets of society, but that doesn't mean every place is like that."

A few minutes later, when Rosalind brought out his burger, he settled in to eat it. "Now, if you could give me directions on how to get to the animal clinic, that would be very helpful."

"Sure."

Old Joe handed Conall a piece of paper, as he ate. Once he had it in his head, he nodded. "Okay, good enough. I'll check it out, when I get through with my lunch here."

"Do I need to warn my daughter?" the waitress asked hesitantly.

He frowned again and shook his head. "I'm only here to talk to them. We're not accusing anybody of anything." He didn't say it, but it was obvious that she heard something in his voice.

"She would never do anything to hurt an animal," she declared.

"I'm not expecting to find anybody at the clinic who hurt any animal, including this War Dog," Conall clarified. "I just don't know what happened to it, and I don't have any leads, and I need to find out on my own, without dealing with people distorting events or mixing up memories."

He sensed something between Old Joe and Rosalind, a silent communication or something, but Conall also knew that he was an outsider. Having declared who and what he was and why he was here, he was even more of an outsider, particularly if they knew something about the missing dog. "It would, however, be really helpful if anybody who knows something about the missing War Dog would speak up," Conall suggested.

"What will you do then?" Rosalind asked, her gaze narrowing. "You don't know that anything bad has happened to that dog."

He raised his eyebrows. "No, I sure don't," he agreed, "but I also don't know that anything *good* has happened. So, until I get to the bottom of this, I'll be checking it out." He got up, put down the money for the bill, including a decent tip, then walked slowly toward the front door. His limp would show, mostly because he'd been sitting for a while.

Old Joe called out, "Good luck."

Conall had little doubt what that meant, as he lifted a hand in reply and stepped outside. Sure enough, there he found the same gang of hoodlums who had raised the stink about the coffee, before he'd taken a picture of their truck.

He looked at them for a long moment, then slowly walked to his vehicle. He knew exactly what their reaction would be to his limp.

The bullies recognized it right away, and they started jeering.

Old Joe came out and swore at them. "You leave him alone," he roared. "He served our nation and did tours in the military. You never signed up, so you don't know a damn thing about what happened to him."

"Don't matter if I do or not," Jake howled, "but he walks like some stiff robot."

"Only until the joint eases off," Conall stated, having heard it all before. After a few more steps, his muscles had eased enough that he could walk a lot more normally. He looked at Jake intently. "Guess you've never been badly injured, *huh*?"

"No, sure haven't. Only losers get injured," he declared, with a laugh.

"Interesting point," Conall replied. "So, you don't know anybody who's been injured who isn't a loser, *huh*?"

"No, nobody I know of that isn't a loser." He glanced at the other two men with him. "What about you guys? You don't know anybody who's not a loser who's been injured, do you?"

One of his buddies looked uncomfortable.

Conall nodded. "It's one thing to be following an ass, but it's another thing when it hits a little more personally, isn't it?"

The guy just glared at him.

"This injured person in your life, what would he think of your judgment of him?"

At that, Jake laughed. "That's his father, and he's a loser anyway."

"Hey, that's not fair," the burly guy protested.

"Hell, you know this guy's a loser too." Jake pointed at Conall, with a sneer. "He joined the military and look what happened to him. He ended up looking like this."

Old Joe snorted. "So? It wasn't his fault."

"It is his fault if he made the stupid decision to go into the military," Jake added, with another jeer.

The other guy's face flushed with anger, but he didn't do

anything.

"A bully never stops unless you stand up to him," Conall told the guy.

At that, the guy turned on him and glared. "You don't know anything."

"I don't need to," Conall stated, without being intimidated or showing any anger. Why give them ammunition? "I can see it all from here."

"Yeah? What do you see?" Jake snapped.

"That you guys are pieces of shit. You walk around town, don't pay for anything, take from these people, and you abuse them. About the abuse though, I think you verbally abuse everybody around you because you're so insignificant and insecure that it's the only way you can face yourself in the morning. You only feel like a big man if you make the others around you seem to be smaller, by verbally beating up on everybody around you."

There was dead silence all around.

Conall noted that Rosalind had joined Old Joe outside. They had stepped out so they could hear Conall. He walked over to his vehicle, then stopped and looked back at them. "The name's Conall, so ..."

Jake jumped in to add, "So, when we need the name for your gravestone?"

"Are you threatening me?" Conall asked, with a small smile in Jake's direction, giving him a lazy look, up and down.

"What are you gonna do about it?"

"First off, it'll take more than you *boys* to worry me. But now that you have threatened me in public, in front of everybody, I've got absolutely no qualms about putting you six feet under, if you try to physically attack me." He smiled at the bullies, taunting them.

He got in his vehicle, raised a hand at Old Joe, and said, "Thanks for lunch," and, with that, he drove away.

"HE DID WHAT?" Bethany Wittaker asked her mother in horror. She stared down at the phone. "Somebody braced those idiots? Why would he have taken them seriously in the first place?" She was shocked, looking for a reason, stumbling on her words.

As she listened to her mother's explanation, Bethany shook her head. "So, he's injured? That's not good."

Her mom rattled on about thinking that maybe he was a veteran himself.

"Sure, but you also know those punks are bad news, and the fact that Jake came after your place again just drives me nuts."

"I know, but we can't do anything about it, at least not personally. He and his crew are too slimy for us to even deal with," she muttered.

"I know, but thanks for the heads-up on the War Dog," she muttered. She hung up the phone, staring down at it.

"What was that all about?"

She looked over at Adam, her part-time employee, and shook her head. "Somebody is here about the War Dog, or will be here soon anyway."

"We were expecting that," he said, with a shrug, "so, that's not exactly newsworthy."

"No, but he stopped by Joe's Diner, and Jake and his boys were there, giving the place a shakedown again, not paying as usual."

"That kid is just a piece of shit."

"I know, but nobody ever tells him that. ... Apparently this new guy made no bones about it, and they got into quite a discussion that turned into Jake threatening him."

"Threatening him?"

"Yeah, and in front of everybody at that."

"Which won't make a damn bit of difference if just his friends were there," he pointed out. "As you and I both know, Jake has a habit of getting away with all the crap he pulls."

"Isn't that the truth," she agreed bitterly. "In this case, the guy stated that now that Jake had threatened him publicly, he would have absolutely no remorse about taking him down, should Jake ever attack him."

At that, Adam whistled. "That would have been a shock to Jake's ego. He's run pretty wild around this place, and nobody's ever threatened him back."

"I don't even think it was a threat," she clarified. "It sounded more like a promise, at least according to Mom."

"Dramatics aside, it's pretty amazing that anybody even stood up to Jake." Adam chuckled at the thought.

"Yeah, but you know somebody has to. That kid has run wild for far too long."

"Agreed. Just because his daddy owns so much property here doesn't mean that Jake should do what he does."

"I agree with you. It's just a sad day when a stranger comes to town on a completely different issue, one I'm already not too thrilled about, and here we end up with him getting a really bad impression of this place right off the bat."

"I don't think it's a bad impression. It's probably a true impression. You and I both know Jake's gotten even harder and harder to deal with over the years. Thankfully, because of the work we do, we don't have to deal with him much."

"Maybe not," she conceded, rotating her neck, "but it does seem he's getting more out of control. If somebody doesn't do something soon, it'll be bad news for everybody involved."

"You and I both know that's exactly what it'll be, bad news all the way. So, if Jake got put in his place by somebody, … I say it's all good."

"Yeah, and what if he turns around and hurts this guy? He came here because of the War Dog," she shared. "So, it'll hardly do us any good if he gets attacked here because of that punk."

"Even if that happened, it wouldn't be our fault," Adam pointed out, shaking his head. "It's not as if we would have anything to do with it."

Just then the receptionist, Melanie, came into the back. "A man is here to talk to you about the missing War Dog," she announced, her voice rising in excitement.

Bethany shook her head at her receptionist. "It's fine, Mel. I'll go talk to him."

Shooting a glance at Adam, she headed out to the waiting room. Once there, she stopped and frowned. There he was, just as her mom had described. Bethany stepped forward and asked, "May I help you?"

# CHAPTER 2

BETHANY STEPPED FARTHER into the waiting room. The man turned and looked at her, and that gaze pinned her on the spot. She immediately wanted to tell him the truth about absolutely everything in her world, not that she was normally a liar, but this guy was something else.

He nodded. "Hi," he greeted her, with a polite smile. "I'm Conall, and I'm here about a War Dog that you checked over a while back."

She nodded. "I'm Dr. Bethany Wittaker. I did, and he was in decent shape."

"I'm sure glad to hear that. Apparently you released Bacchus to somebody other than Michael."

She shrugged. "I released him for sure, to someone I thought to be the nephew at the time. We had a letter stating so. We have dealt with this dog many times in the past, but the owner ..." She paused and thought about it, searching for the right words. "I'm not sure I've ever seen him, so it was a very common thing for him to send others in to drop off and to pick up Bacchus."

"Do you know anything or have you heard anything as to how the dog went missing?"

"I probably know less than you do," she admitted, shrugging. "We heard that he never arrived home, but that's all. The only reason I know that much is that Michael called to see where Bacchus was. I told him that he'd been released to his nephew. Then he started to get angry, saying his nephew was there and had been all afternoon."

"Do you have any reason to doubt Michael's story?"

"No, not at all, but there is also no reason for you to think that I did something to the dog either," she stated. "I'm not sure what's going on or who would want to take the dog." She shook her head. "That just makes no sense to me at all."

"No, of course not," he murmured. "And I'm here to get the facts, not to blame the clinic."

She looked at him with an assessing gaze. "Do you have any reason to suspect that Bacchus would have been stolen?"

"Not any reason to suspect anything at this point," he noted. "I have to find out all I can about what happened, and that could provide all kinds of different leads, but I thought I would start with where he went missing from."

She pondered that and shrugged. "He might have gone missing from here, but I really can't be sure because he was picked up and led outside. I didn't see the vehicle or even the man himself, for that matter."

"And that's a critical point," Conall noted, with a searching gaze. "Who released the dog?"

Bethany turned and called out, "Mel, can you come here, please?"

The younger woman stepped out, nervously wiping her hands on her jeans. "Hi," she said sheepishly.

"This man wants to know who you released the dog to."

She flushed. "I don't know."

"What do you mean, you don't know?" Bethany asked, frowning.

"I had the letter, and I brought the dog out. No medication, no special instructions or anything had to be handed out," she explained, "and it was a really busy day." She glanced over at her boss, frowning. "Remember? We had dogs here, dogs there." Mel fumbled, pointing to the area around them. "Then a cat got loose, and all kinds of chaos happened."

"Oh, right. I remember that now." Bethany winced.

"So, when you turned around, the dog was gone. Is that it?" Conall asked Mel.

"Yes."

"So, you don't know whether the dog went with anybody or just managed to get out the open door, is that it?" Conall asked specifically.

"I brought him out for somebody"—Mel frowned—"but the dog was just over here, lying on the floor, waiting. So … I didn't even see who picked him up."

"How did you know to get him ready?"

"We'd gotten a phone call, and then there was the letter on the desk." She stopped and added, "That seems very strange, doesn't it?"

"Yeah, it seems very strange." Bethany groaned. "Okay, so maybe we have a little more to do with this than I would like," she muttered, glancing at her employee.

"So, you never saw who took Bacchus or spoke to anyone *in person*?" Conall confirmed.

"No," Mel confessed. "I'm sorry. It was just crazy that day."

"I remember," Bethany muttered. "You're right. It was a bad day in many ways." She turned to Conall. "Is it paranoid to suggest that somebody may have been intentionally causing issues? I'm beginning to wonder if maybe somebody did take him," she admitted.

"Maybe," Conall replied. "It still sounds a little odd to think it would have worked out so perfectly."

"Or they just came in, saw the dog there, he jumped up to greet them, and just walked out with them?" Bethany suggested. "Bacchus is a very friendly dog."

"I was away from my desk for," Mel explained, pondering it, "maybe … ten minutes, fifteen tops, trying to restore order, with the cat on the loose and the dogs freaking out everywhere."

"So, there is a gap in the timeline then. When did you find out there was a problem?" Conall asked her.

"As I remember, Michael called me later that day," Bethany replied, "and it was after business hours because I answered it from home. I told him to let me know if the dog didn't return afterward. Then I didn't hear anything for at least a week. By then our security tapes had been overwritten, since we only keep them for three days."

Conall nodded. "So, nobody has a clue whether the dog just took off or someone picked him up." He pondered the information. "How far away was he from home?"

"Not far at all, maybe five blocks," Bethany noted, and then she nodded. "You're right. Bacchus may well have just gone on home then."

"He would have under normal circumstances, … yes," Conall stated.

"You don't think this was a normal circumstance, do you?" Bethany asked.

"Do you?" he asked, with a wry look.

She flushed and then shook her head. "Maybe not, but I honestly don't know what to tell you."

He stared at her for a long moment, then his gaze switched to Melanie.

Mel immediately went into broken-record mode. "I'm sorry. I'm so sorry. I don't know what to tell you. I was trying to catch the cat, and the dogs were after her. We had two people in the waiting room, and they were lingering around with their dogs. … I did try to hold back their animals. I mean, anybody could have stepped in, picked up the dog, and walked out," she muttered. "I didn't even think about it, but I was expecting the dog to be picked up. So, when I realized he was gone, I just thought, *Oh, good, one less thing to worry about*, and off I went."

"*Off you went*," Conall muttered.

Mel flushed. "Yeah, and I don't mean that in a bad way, but …" She fell silent, looking miserable.

"And who were the two people in the waiting room?" he asked.

Mel just grimaced, then said, "I'm not sure."

He shifted to look at Bethany.

She shrugged. "Mel, check the schedule for that day and give those names to the investigator."

Mel frowned. "I can try. I'm not sure how to get into the calendar and go backward."

Bethany shrugged. "Mel, try to get it done." She turned to Conall and added, "I'll follow up."

Conall stood here for a long moment, as if pondering his options and the information he'd been given. Then with a nod, he said, "I'll be back."

And, with that, he headed out.

# CHAPTER 3

BETHANY NOTICED HIS gait shifting with every movement, as he headed out to his vehicle.

"What's wrong with his leg?" Mel asked.

Bethany shrugged. "Looks like he's got a prosthetic."

"Oh, wow." Excitement filled her voice, as if she'd never seen anybody with such a thing. It just belied her age and inexperience, and that literally summed up what this had been, a failure on their part. Even if nobody else would acknowledge it, Bethany would because no way that dog should have been handed off without signatures and at least recognition that one specific person was here to pick him up.

Bethany had seen the dog multiple times, and they had a decent rapport, but she was still a vet, and he would not necessarily see her as his best buddy, which was too bad in a way, because she absolutely loved animals. She walked outside where Conall was getting into his vehicle and called out to him to wait. "I'm sorry. I didn't realize just how bad that all sounded, until I listened to my assistant. She's new. She's green and obviously inexperienced."

He asked, "There's just her?"

Bethany winced. "She's here almost full-time. I have a surgical assistant as needed, plus a part-time employee in the back right now, cleaning cages and feeding the animals. We're currently short-staffed, like everybody in town, with its dying economy. People working for us before just quit or decided to go do something else," she explained, with a sigh. "Staffing has been a huge issue."

He just nodded at that.

"Anyway, if we can come up with any more information, we'll definitely send it your way. I just don't know what else I can tell you."

"Just don't make up anything," Conall stated. "The truth is always the best answer."

"No need to tell me about the truth," she replied defensively. "If I don't have anything to give you, ... there's nothing more I can do."

"Just tell me that you don't know anything about Bacchus," he said, "then I can carry on from here." He stopped and stared at her. "You look like Rosalind."

She flushed, then laughed. "She's my mother. I gather you were at the coffee shop."

He nodded. "And I gather that you were informed about my arrival." She lowered her head because he was certainly right about that. "What about this Jake character who keeps shaking them down for free coffee?"

A glint of anger slid into her expression and her tone, as she muttered, "There's three or four of them, and Jake's always been a bully. He's a user and a loser," she stated, "and they just keep targeting my mom's place."

"And Joe?"

She shrugged. "My mom and Old Joe have been an item for years." She smiled. "My father died when I was about eight, and Joe's just been there in the background. If they're happy, I don't have a problem with it." She hated the defensiveness that rose in her tone at the mention of her mother's relationship.

"Everybody is entitled to companionship and happiness," Conall stated. "It's nobody's place to judge where they find it."

She nodded. "I agree with you there, but not everybody is that open-minded."

He eyed her for a moment. "But what's the problem?"

She shrugged. "I'm not sure there's a problem, as much as people just look down on him because they run the café, and, of course, he's black."

"Since when is having a little cafeteria a negative?" he asked in wonder. "I would have thought it was a fairly common profession all across the country. And black, white, yellow shouldn't make a damn bit of difference."

"Exactly, and my mom used to work for an insurance company, at least until she got fired a few years ago. That's when she started working with Old Joe."

"Why did your mom get fired?"

"According to the townsfolk, she'd been stealing money, but she hadn't," Bethany declared, glaring at him.

"Stealing?" He shook his head. "No, I can't see her doing that."

She stared at him in astonishment. "It's not as if you really know her. You had coffee at her shop for what, about five minutes?"

He shrugged. "I'm pretty good at judging character," he murmured, "which is also why I don't like those punks."

"You and the rest of the town, but Jake's daddy owns the mill. So Jake thinks he can get away with anything."

"He thinks it because he has gotten away with it." Conall shook his head. "Somebody needs to clean Jake's clock a time or two and make him realize he's not the big shot that he thinks he is."

"He's nothing," she agreed, "but nobody will buck him because of his father, because the mill is the biggest employer here, supporting most of the townsfolk. He owns the mill and, hell, most of the area, for that matter. Anyone who messes with Jake, the next thing you hear is, … they're fired," she shared, with loathing in her tone. "It's that easy."

"Any other industries coming in?" he asked, looking around.

"No, it's become more of a sleepy town than anything, and the mill is the last frontier in terms of work."

"And yet there's work not very far away, correct?"

"Sure, if you don't mind driving to the next town."

He looked down the road. "What is that, about half an hour?"

She smiled. "Yes, half an hour," she confirmed, "and a lot of people do work there. We're trying to stop everybody from moving away. Otherwise my business will go belly up too," she noted, turning to look back at the vet clinic.

"But you could also move to the next town and survive just fine if you had to, right?" he asked her.

"I could, and I might if it becomes necessary." She glanced back at him. "But that's hardly your issue, is it?"

"No, not my issue at all," he agreed, with a smile, "but I like problems, and this problem's right up my alley."

"What kind of problem is that?" she asked, frowning at him. "Revitalization?"

"Revitalization? Nope. *Bullies.*" And, with that, he closed the door of his truck and started the engine.

She stepped back and watched as he pulled away. Something was unique about him, yet she was damn sure that Jake and his gang of ruffians would run all over him.

As Conall pulled the vehicle around to head toward the

open road, she added, "You watch yourself. Those guys are bad news, and they'll stab you in the back, laughing while they do it."

He eyed her for a long moment. "Have they done something like that to anybody?"

"I don't know," she admitted, with a shrug. "A couple incidents happened not all that long ago, and we have no idea whether they were behind it or not."

"What about law enforcement?"

"We don't have any here in town anymore. We're not big enough," she said. "The nearest thing we have is a sheriff's office the next town over. Yet it doesn't matter, as Jake's father is a stereotypical deep-pocket friend of law enforcement."

"I don't care how friendly they are," Conall snapped. "Law enforcement can be dirty too."

She nodded. "But there again, most people aren't up for the fight."

"Yeah? If I get into a fight," Conall stated, "I make sure it's one I can win. Sometimes these fights are the kind you just can't lose because you've got to do what's right, no matter what. You've got to face yourself in the mirror every morning, and it doesn't matter what punks like these are doing with their lives. They've got to be stopped."

With that said, he drove off.

CONALL WASN'T EXACTLY sure what made him declare such an interest in this issue, and he certainly wasn't of a mind to go down that pathway, but sometimes you just had to figure out the right and wrong of it, and he could see that Old Joe and Rosalind were ones who would take a hit here, all because these punks thought they had a right to cause trouble. That would never sit well in Conall's world. He understood bullies like them and had dealt with the type before. What Conall knew for certain was that the bullies wouldn't ever stop, not until somebody put a stop to it.

He headed to the only motel in town, registered for a couple nights, then drove toward Michael's place. As Conall got out and headed up to the front door, a younger male, who he assumed was the nephew, opened the door and glared at him. Conall silently waited.

The nephew, seeming almost unnerved, snapped, "What are you doing here?"

Conall raised his eyebrows. "Any idea who I am?" he asked.

"I thought you were somebody specific, but maybe you're not." He frowned. "Who are you, and what are you doing here?"

At the very chilly and even angry greeting, he shook his head. "I'm Conall, and I'm here about the War Dog that went missing."

"Oh." The nephew looked completely flabbergasted. "You seriously came here for a War Dog?"

Conall smiled and nodded. "Yes, I came for a War Dog."

"Jeez, don't you guys have anything better to do with your time?"

"Use of my time isn't something that concerns you," he stated, staring at the younger man. "I've got a question for you. If it wasn't you who went to pick up the War Dog, who did?"

"I don't know," he snapped. "I've got better things to do

than worry about that dog."

"And what would those *better things* be?" Conall asked, studying the nephew. There wasn't any guile about him, but there also wasn't anything that made Conall think this guy was citizen-of-the-year-award material either.

"Look. My uncle has a lot of health issues, so I'm constantly looking after him. Don't have time for babysitting a dog too."

"Your uncle might have some health issues," Conall noted, "but I highly doubt that he needs twenty-four-hour care. Otherwise he would be in a place where they could give it to him."

"Maybe he doesn't want that," he declared, staring at him. "What do you know about it anyway?"

"I don't know anything … yet," Conall replied, with a lazy smile. "Some of you guys were pissing me off today, and I can't decide how involved I want to get."

"Don't get involved with anybody here," he declared. "You'll end up in battles you can't afford to win."

"*Hmm*, maybe it will be more of a case of battles I can't afford to lose," he clarified, studying him. "So, where is your uncle now?"

"He's resting."

"I would like to talk to him."

"You can't, at least not now. He's resting."

"Okay, and when will he *not* be resting?" Somehow, Conall knew the answer would be one he wouldn't like.

"That's not happening."

Conall nodded. "That's very interesting," he noted, with a smirk, "but that's the expected answer, isn't it?"

"Look. We don't want any trouble."

At that, with a searching gaze, Conall looked around,

then at the nephew. "Trouble from whom?"

He flushed. "You've come with a bit of trouble already, and we don't need any of that."

"What kind of trouble did I come with?"

"We heard about your argument at Joe's Diner," he shared, red in the face, "and we can't afford to get involved with trouble like that."

"What kind of trouble do you think I got into?" he asked in amazement.

The nephew didn't say anything, but he now looked around nervously.

From inside the house, a man called out, "Page, let him in, damn it. You know I need to talk to him."

Page glared back and called out, "No, he'll just cause trouble."

"Sounds to me that you've already got trouble," Conall stated. "Are you really thinking I'll bring more in?"

"Yeah, you already have," Page snapped.

"I didn't tell anybody I was coming here. I didn't even tell anybody but Rosalind and Old Joe what I was doing in town."

"No, but then you went to the animal clinic and talked to Mel and Bethany."

"Ah, don't tell me," Conall said, understanding the hesitation and resistance now. "You're sweet on Melanie, *huh*?"

Page flushed. "She's my girl, okay?"

"So, as soon as I left there, she called you, is that it?"

His face turned bright red. "You can't get her in trouble for that."

"I'm not so sure," Conall noted, with an unnerving smile. "It will be interesting to see how her boss feels about that."

"Oh, no you don't," he roared. "That's not fair."

"Neither is broadcasting information that's not your business." Conall brushed past the nephew and stepped into the living room.

"I didn't say you could go in there."

"You didn't need to. Your uncle told me that I could come in here." He walked through until he saw an old man sitting in the living room in a wheelchair, a blanket thrown over his legs. Conall smiled and said, "Hi, my name's Conall."

The old man eyed him with a shrewd gaze. "Which division?"

He smiled. "Navy SEALs."

The old man's scowl disappeared. "I was Navy too." Then he provided his credentials.

Conall nodded. "Very pleased to meet you, sir."

"Damn, it's good to see somebody who knows something. Pull up a chair, son. We've got to talk."

"So, what are we talking about?" Conall asked, as he pulled up a chair and glanced back over at Page, standing in the doorway, clearly disgruntled. "Your nephew doesn't want me here."

"Of course not, he doesn't want any trouble, and his girlfriend already called to let us know you were coming," Michael confirmed, with a laugh. "As if that'll make a damn bit of difference. I told him that we wouldn't shake you."

"Of course not," Conall agreed. "I wouldn't be doing the job then, would I?"

"No, you sure wouldn't be." Michael gave a big sigh of satisfaction and smiled. "So, I was right."

"Sounds like it."

"You want a beer?" he offered.

Conall shrugged. "No thanks."

At that, the nephew turned, as if understanding that the uncle would insist on it anyway. When Page came back, he brought Conall a lukewarm can.

With a shrug, he popped the top and sat here and sipped it with the old man. "Now, you tell me. What the hell is going on here?"

Michael groaned. "I'm not sure." He gave Conall a shrewd look. "Ever since my nephew came to stay with me, Bacchus started to disappear more and more in the daytime."

Michael gave his nephew a calculating look. "For a while there I thought maybe my nephew was having problems with him. Sometimes dogs just take a dislike to somebody in particular, and I didn't really understand what was going on," Michael admitted, waving his hands, "but I watched them together, and there didn't seem to be any issue. Yet, every damn time Bacchus went outside, he came back a little bit later and later."

"Any injuries?"

"He always came back in good shape, so it's not as if anybody was abusing him. He always seemed to be happy enough. I just didn't have any explanation, but neither could I really get out there and track him down. I did ask Page here to follow him a couple times, and he always lost him, as if the dog were deliberately trying to avoid him."

At that, knowing his disbelief showed in his expression, Conall glanced over at the nephew, who was flushing bright red. "*Right*. That'll be an interesting conversation to have with your nephew."

Page immediately blustered, "I didn't do anything to that damn dog."

"Neither did you track him down, as you said you

would," Conall countered in a monotone. "You just lied to your uncle here and figured it was *just a dog*. Who gave a crap, right?"

Michael frowned at his nephew, then cried out to Conall, "What?"

Conall looked over at the nephew. "You want to tell Michael the truth for a change, or do you think that the old man doesn't deserve even that much respect?"

"I didn't say that," Page roared. "Don't you go putting words in my mouth."

Michael turned and looked at his nephew in disbelief. "Did you lie to me? Did you not even go looking for my dog?"

"Look. You didn't need the dog anyway, and he kept walking away. I mean, if he doesn't want to be here, he doesn't want to be here."

"Damn." Michael stared at his nephew in consternation. "And when were you gonna tell me that?"

"I wasn't," he snapped. "That damn dog was missing. He was happy to be missing, so whatever. Nobody knows what the hell has happened to it now, and nobody's seen it, so what do you care?"

"I care," Michael bellowed, almost roaring himself now, "because he is my responsibility." Michael immediately started fretting, lifting and dropping the blanket in front of him, as if trying to figure out his next course of action.

Conall reached out a hand, patting his. "I'll go look for him. That's what I'm here for."

Michael stilled and looked up at him, peering in closer to see if he could really trust him, and then nodded. "I need to know that I can trust you."

"I'm here for the dog. I'm not here for you," he stated

pointedly. "But, if I can help you while I'm here, I'm okay to do that too." Reaching out, he shook Michael's hand. "I have no time to clear anyone's conscience, but rest assured. I'm here for Bacchus."

"Good," Michael muttered, settling down. "Good, that's what's important." Then he turned and glared at his nephew. "We need to have a talk, boy."

His nephew just shrugged.

"Seems a complete lack of respect is here," Conall muttered to the older man, as he faced Michael. "Are you sure you want him here living with you?"

Michael frowned at him, his gaze shrewd. "Not always a whole lot of choice when you get old."

"Ah." Conall nodded. Then he glanced back at the nephew, who walked out, slamming the door behind him.

"So, is he getting room and board to look after you or just free room and board until you die?"

The old man winced. "You call a spade a spade," he declared, with a chuckle. "I've got to respect that. As for Page, well, … I think you're probably right."

"He's got a girlfriend, you know? … And it doesn't look to me as if they're planning on sticking around for all that long."

Michael nodded, as he stared off in the distance, "Really ain't a whole lot left for people like me, when you get old. I was hoping Page would be a companion, hoping he would be there for me a little more," he admitted. "But he's a young man, with his life to live, and I guess looking after his old uncle isn't exactly the kind of life he was expecting."

"No, I don't imagine it was. Did he think you had money?"

Michael stared at him and swallowed. "I wouldn't be at

all surprised if he suspected that, but I don't," he replied. "I've got my pension, and that's it."

"Are you keeping the pension for yourself or are you sharing it with him?"

He flushed. "He has asked a couple times for some money. … I'm not paying him to be here, so I kind of feel bad when he doesn't have much of a life and …"

Michael fumbled to explain, and Conall could see that. "Yeah, but he could still get a job and be here for you too."

Michael nodded. "I did suggest that, but he's not big on the idea."

"Why is that?"

Michael gave a crack of laughter. "The same reason all these other young'uns don't want to get a job—because work is required. At the end of the day, you don't get a paycheck for doing nothing."

Conall nodded. "Seems to be a blight on a lot of people these days."

"Isn't that the truth? I don't know. … I did talk to my sister about him, and Page got into trouble where he was, you know. He dipped his hand into the cash register, where he was working. They recovered the money, so they didn't press charges and just opted to get rid of him."

"So, she got rid of him too, by sending him off to you."

"Yeah, yeah," he agreed glumly.

"So, we already know who got the worst part of that deal." Conall smiled. "Yet you're not completely alone, and maybe it's worth it to you."

"I don't know," he muttered. "Maybe. I really have no idea. I keep thinking about it, but it's hardly turned out the way I'd hoped. Especially now that Bacchus is missing. And damn that boy for not looking for the dog as he was supposed to."

"You don't have any other family? Nobody you could stay with?"

"No, no other family, just a sister, and she's …" He stopped, as if searching for right words. "She's kind of a mess."

"And she's dealing with him too, isn't she?"

"Yeah, and that's part of the mess," Michael confirmed, with a smile. "She hasn't had a husband for a while, and the boy didn't have a strong upbringing. Of course I tend to think that I'm still a strong influence, but I'm sure all they see is the cripple in the wheelchair. So, for whatever reason, any respect goes right out the window."

"Maybe so, but it shouldn't," Conall stated. "That's got absolutely nothing to do with it, but, because you also feel as if you've got nothing left to give, it comes across that way."

"It sure does," he said, with a nod. "I got cornered in the parking lot by that stupid punk kid," he shared, shaking his head, "and I haven't really been out much since."

Conall frowned. "You mean Jake and his cohorts?"

"Oh, you've already met them, have you?" Michael cackled. "They're just no damn good."

"Yeah, I got that impression, and they sure as hell shouldn't be harassing our veterans."

"Yeah, but nobody has any respect anymore. They think you went to war because you were some sort of fool, whom everybody else has to pay the price for," he muttered. "Nobody cares, and it's a sad, lonely world at this stage." His voice had dropped so low, and Michael had looked so lost, it was almost as if he were talking to himself.

Conall didn't know what to say to that, though he was in the same boat, just younger. Yet there were so many similarities that he could certainly relate to. "So, this War Dog," he asked, "what is his temperament like?"

"He's a big baby and loves everybody," Michael shared, with a chuckle.

"So, there is a chance then that somebody may have picked him up on the road and just taken him along because he was a big teddy bear?"

"It's possible, but everybody local knew he was mine," Michael said, "but now that I hear what my nephew apparently didn't say, maybe he knows more than he's telling me."

"It sounds like he definitely knows more than he's telling," Conall confirmed. "What will it take to get him to tell the truth?"

Michael looked over at him. "I just need a bit of time, and he'll probably come clean," he muttered, "but I can't guarantee it. I would hope so because I would like to think we have a better relationship than what he's demonstrating right now. It does break my heart to think that Bacchus might be with somebody he doesn't like."

"And, if he was with somebody he *did* like, how would you feel?"

"I would be okay with it, if he didn't want to be with me," he shared, with a sad smile. "Obviously I'm lonely but okay. Been there, done that, I guess. I just never really expected to have a War Dog who didn't get along with me."

"Of course not," Conall replied, "and I'm not saying he didn't. I'm just saying that maybe something else may have appealed or *somebody* else may have appealed, and maybe Page was enough of a reason for Bacchus to not want to stay with you. Or maybe staying with you was something Bacchus felt he needed to do while you were alone, and then, once you weren't alone anymore, maybe that changed."

"*Huh*." Michael stared at him. "I hadn't considered any of that, and I honestly had believed Bacchus had a great relationship with my nephew."

Conall looked at him with half a smile. "And now that you can see that your nephew lied to you about not following the dog, you can see that there wouldn't likely be any kind of relationship there."

"And that's wrong too," he muttered, with a nod. "Just as Page doesn't respect my days of military service, he also doesn't respect any that the War Dog put in either, and that's a damn shame."

Conall silently agreed with him. "What about Bethany, the veterinarian? How do you feel about her?"

"She's always been good to see to the dog. I'm not sure what else to say because that's where his girlfriend works, Melanie or something like that. If my nephew had been there, she would have seen him, and they would have probably been making eyes at each other, before he picked up the dog and brought him home."

"Apparently some chaos happened at the vet clinic at the time, so Bacchus had been out near the reception area, waiting for your nephew to pick him up. There was a letter saying that he was picking him up. So, are you saying that you sent your nephew?"

"He told me that he couldn't go, but now I don't know what to say."

"Sounds to me as if a lot of lies and some BS is going on. Page went down there and either handed him off to somebody else, or maybe he just didn't pick up Bacchus, and the dog got loose. I can totally imagine Page trying to cover it up, and it seems maybe the girlfriend was probably spending way more time focused on Page instead of her job. So, who knows? Maybe that's how Bacchus got loose."

Michael stared at him. "It's a damn shame, but it's quite likely to have happened that way or close to it," he admitted. "The question is, what do we do about it now?"

"That's the trick, isn't it? Because now I've got to find a dog that either got ushered out the door into the big world on his own and may or may not have decided *not* to return to you. It may boil down to just your nephew, who didn't want to bring Bacchus home. And the most important question is, where is the dog now?"

"Wouldn't we all like to know?" Michael said, as he stared at the doorway, where his nephew had disappeared through. "Now I've got to figure out what to do about Page."

"Send him back to his mother," Conall stated, without even having to think about it. "He's not your problem, and, if he won't respect you, then he won't respect her either."

"Yeah, but he needs a firm hand."

Conall studied Michael intently. "And is that your job?"

"No, it's not my job. I'm not sure it's anybody's job now. Page is an adult, and I don't know what I'm supposed to do anymore." He rubbed his temples. "He was a good kid at one time. He's still a good kid. He's just lost right now."

As he stood up, Conall said, "Sometimes people need to find their own way, or they stay lost forever." He put his empty beer can on the coffee table beside him and reached out to shake Michael's hand. "Thanks for the beer."

"Are you coming back?"

"I'll come back," he stated, with a smile, "but I've got to find out some things first."

"What's that?"

"I've got to get to the bottom of the lies," he replied.

"That's a good start."

"After that, I'm not too sure," Conall admitted. "No relevant security camera footage remains at the clinic because it was all overwritten."

"You think the girl at that clinic did that?"

"I'm not sure," he replied. "Melanie acted very scattered, blaming it on a busy day."

"Yeah? I guess she is a good match for Page," he muttered, with a groan. "Too bad because what he needs is somebody level-headed who'll kick his butt out to get to work."

"That's not likely to happen," Conall noted, with a smile. "You and I both know that."

"And yet I was kind of hoping it would be a good match."

"I'm not saying it isn't a good match, but a good match starts with honesty."

And, on that note, he got up and walked out.

# CHAPTER 4

Bethany stepped out of the building at the end of the day, tired and a little worn out. She turned to lock up, only to find the man who had been in her thoughts all day standing there, waiting for her. She startled, then frowned. "Did you find out something already?"

"I found out that Page was to pick up Bacchus that day and that the written message never came from Michael, probably never reached your assistant. Have you ever seen the supposed note?"

She stared at him in surprise, with a sinking feeling in her heart. "Well, crap, so you're thinking she lied?"

He nodded. "I'm thinking she lied. What I really need to know is, would she do that, if it meant protecting her and her boyfriend?"

"Absolutely. I've had to get after her a couple times, and I've asked him not to come by during working hours, unless she's off for lunch."

"Ah." Conall nodded. "So there's a good chance that's what happened. You both mentioned there was some extra chaos at the time?"

"Yes," she admitted. "Mel didn't secure the latch on one of the cat cages, so the cat got out, and two dogs were in the waiting room, right outside of the checkup room."

"And the minute you have a cat on the run in front of

some dogs, chaos ensues, creating a plausible explanation."

"Sure, but not one I would be happy with, if she lied—or if letting out the cat had been deliberate."

"Can you get the truth out of her?"

She winced. "I'm not sure if I can. She's one of those people who tends to double down when she's caught in her lies."

"*Great*," he muttered, as he stared around them. "Cases like this that start with lies end up with more lies."

She nodded. "I was really hoping that wouldn't be the case. Bacchus is wonderful. I really hope he's okay."

"I just had a long talk with Michael, and Page was there for a while, until it got a little too uncomfortable for him. Apparently he told the old man that he followed the dog, as asked multiple times, when he didn't."

"So, he lied to his uncle?" she asked in horror.

"Yeah, he sure did. He was supposed to be following Bacchus to solve the mystery of where he was disappearing to. He gave his uncle some BS story and didn't follow Bacchus at all. Then I found out from Michael that Page was sent to pick up the dog, and yet somehow that didn't happen either. And the story of this letter to say that the nephew was supposed to pick him up was bogus, when no letter was needed."

Bethany frowned. "What are you thinking now?"

He shrugged. "A couple liars were involved. That's what I'm thinking. I'm guessing, one way or another, they screwed up and lost the dog—or worse. Then they needed to cover it up. So they made up a story on the run and thought, *Oh, well, one missing dog, but who cares?* Right?"

"But it's a War Dog," she clarified.

"Sure, it's a War Dog, a dog who has already served this

country and who deserves more from us than being dumped on the wayside."

She nodded. "I agree with you there, and we've never charged for his care either, simply because he's a War Dog. He's done his time. He deserves to be looked after, as does his owner."

He nodded. "Do you have any group home facilities here for people like Michael?"

She shook her head. "Not in this town. Some are farther over, but they're government run." She winced. "I shouldn't say it like that, but a lot of times those are pretty rough."

"What about veteran homes?"

"You would know more about that than I would," she replied. "If there was one that Michael wanted to go to, are you thinking Page isn't in it for the long haul?"

"Page is in it for himself, as you should see already, and I wouldn't count on your receptionist sticking around either. I get the sense that they may have some plans of their own."

She flushed, as she stared at him. "I see. We haven't heard anything about her plans around here."

"Maybe not, but based on his attitude and the way he treats his uncle, I would say they've got plans."

"Right," she muttered, with a nod. "Of course they do. It's awfully hard to keep staff around here."

"I'm sure it is. The lure of something bigger and better in another town is always part of the problem."

"It wouldn't be so bad, but not everybody understands and appreciates small-town living. So, when they're born and raised here, they just want to leave," she explained. "I spent a lot of time here, and I came back because this is where my family is, and I hit that stage where family counted, so I had to come back." She smiled over at him. "How about you?

Do you have family nearby?"

"Oh, I've got family," he replied, with half a smile, "but they're off doing research in Europe. My brother works with my parents. They are both chemists, doing a special project in Germany right now."

"Oh, wow," she said. "That sounds pretty amazing."

"They're happy, and that's the biggest thing," Conall stated. "So I don't begrudge them being gone at all."

"Good." She nodded. "There never should be jealousy or greed about somebody else doing well."

"I agree," he muttered. "Now, what will we do about Bacchus?"

She glanced at him. "What is it you expect *me* to do?" she asked in astonishment.

"I'm pretty sure Melanie knows exactly where the War Dog is," he stated, "and, if she knows, I'm willing to bet that you do too."

Her gaze narrowed, as she studied him. Then she shook her head. "You might be right about Mel," she muttered. "However, I don't know where Bacchus has gone, though I keep thinking I have seen him out and about in various places over time, but do I know for sure? *No.* Do I know who Bacchus might have been with? *Hell no.*" He eyed her closely, and she glared back at him. "I don't care whether you believe me or not. What I don't want is you to be thinking that we did something to steal a dog here," she snapped. "That would never be okay in my world."

"So, do you have any idea why the dog was not staying at home with Michael anymore? Why he was taking off on his own?"

She frowned at him and then slowly shook her head. "No, they didn't say anything to us about that. Plus I saw no signs or indications of abuse either."

"If Page was doing the talking, I'm not sure it can be believed, and it sounds like you were getting a good share of your information secondhand. I don't think that nephew of Michael's can be trusted, particularly since we know he's already lied and doesn't seem to think that the truth matters."

She winced. "I don't want to say it's the younger generation," she muttered, "but there is definitely a shift in perception as to what constitutes a lie and what is okay to lie about."

"There has been no such shift or distinction in my book," he declared flatly, "and I don't know if whatever's been going on involves Page or not, but the information we have, so far, certainly doesn't clear him."

"Oh, I get it, and I am not the least bit confused about right or wrong," she muttered, nodding. "I just don't know what you want from me. We can go talk to Melanie and see what she says, I guess. But be prepared, as she's a young girl, and she'll probably go to pieces on you. She may even call the cops."

"She's welcome to call the cops," he said, with a smile. "That'll be one of my stops anyway."

Surprised, she looked at him and asked, "Really?"

He nodded. "Yeah, not only do I have a War Dog missing but also the fact that a young punk is running around terrorizing everybody and being allowed to do so. I find it odd that nobody seems to give a crap about either."

Her temper started to reveal itself at that.

He nodded. "I know you don't like hearing that, but I've only just arrived in town, and I can tell you that's what it looks like from here."

"Sometimes things can be deceptive," she replied, "so don't judge all of us because you're missing a dog."

"I'm not judging anybody," he said, "except maybe the punk because I was there and saw that for myself."

"You were, *huh*?"

He nodded. "I know that your mom probably says it's no big deal, but she's afraid."

At that, Bethany winced. "I don't like the situation at all," she murmured, "and I know that Jake keeps threatening Old Joe. And Old Joe is definitely a force to be reckoned with, but he's not the same when up against a gun."

"Are people packing here? Are those punks armed?"

She nodded. "Most people are nowadays," she muttered. "It's not something that's openly discussed, but, if you watch carefully, a good share of them have ready access to a weapon. Times are changing down here." She shook her head, as she stared around her parking lot, "though I'm not sure it's for the better."

"Of course not," Conall said. "Things are tough enough without having more of that going on. It just raises the stakes when there's trouble. Let's go talk to Melanie. I need some answers and a place to start," he stated, as he looked down at his watch, frowning.

"What? Are you late for a date?"

He flashed her a grin. "Nope, I've only just arrived in town, so haven't had time for that yet," he teased, with a chuckle, "but I am booked at the motel. I'm not sure how early places around here close in terms of hotels, restaurants, and all that."

She shrugged. "No hotels here. Yeah, as far as food, you might want to keep an eye out before too long just because restaurants close early here. We've got time to talk to

Melanie first."

"You know where she lives?"

"Hell, yes." Bethany smiled. "I babysat her when she was growing up."

"Ah, that's another problem with staffing shortages, isn't it?"

"It sure is," she muttered. "Let's get going because I need to get to the bottom of this too. The version she gave me isn't exactly matching what you're saying, and I need to know whether I can trust her or not, since it's my business that's on the line." She pointed at her vehicle. "You can follow me."

And, with that, she hopped into her vehicle and headed out of the clinic's parking lot and down a few blocks, where she took a couple turns to end up in front of Mel's family home. As Bethany got out, she waited for Conall to pull up behind her. She watched him exit the vehicle, noting his leg. "Does that hurt you?" she asked.

He shook his head. "No, though I'm getting used to a new joint." He shrugged. "It works fine most of the time, but it's usually the prosthetic leg that ends up suffering more with the driving. It's been a long day today."

"Ah," she murmured. "Did you come from far away?"

"New Mexico," he replied, with a smile, "so just a few hours. The joint gets stiff, and then it doesn't want to unkink."

"What happened?" she asked bluntly.

"War," he replied equally bluntly.

"Ah, well, I'm sorry to say, but you won't find a whole lot of respect here for that either."

"Yeah, I saw that already," he noted, with a curt smile. "Both Page and Jake were quick to jump on it. Not that I care what any of these punks think, but I won't stand by and let them disrespect the older veterans, who sacrificed so much in the service to their country. It's one thing to object to the decisions that they made and the politics of it all, but these soldiers didn't get a vote in the details of their service. They just followed orders and, in many cases, paid a hell of a price for it."

She nodded. "That's true, and people don't really understand that, myself included," she murmured.

"I know that Michael is a good man. He served his time, and he got pretty beat up over it. I know his PTSD is pretty rough at times too, and honestly the War Dog should have helped in many ways. So I don't know whether he doesn't want the dog or the arrival of the nephew stopped everything from working well."

She looked back at him. "There is another possibility."

"What's that?" he asked, as they walked up to the small one-story rancher, with a bunch of trees all out in the front, blocking most of the view. "What other possibility could there be?"

She hesitated, then turned to him and replied, "Maybe the dog found somebody who needed him more."

CONALL STUDIED HER face carefully. "What is it that you know?"

"I don't know anything," she stated, with a hint of anger in her tone. She didn't appreciate the judgment in his tone. "That's the problem."

Just enough exasperation filled her tone that he believed her. "But you suspect something."

"No, I don't even suspect something. I just know that the dog seemed to have lots of friends around town. He was well-known and well loved." He raised his eyebrows, and she nodded. "He used to go around the parks, homes, on what we call a walkabout, from place to place. The fact that Michael didn't tell you that is a little worrisome."

"I'm not sure that the old boy was in a position to tell me because I'm not sure he knew."

She stared at him. "Seriously?"

He nodded. "Yeah, Michael's wheelchair-bound, doesn't get out of the house much, from what I heard. Plus I suspect the nephew hasn't been telling him very much at all."

She frowned at that. "Why would he do that?"

"Why does anybody do that? Especially when it comes to somebody they're supposed to be helping?"

"You don't think he's helping at all, do you?"

"I really don't know," Conall admitted, "but I'll confess to being a little jaded. I don't know whether Page's just in his own world because he has a girlfriend, and that's all he can think about, or if he's deliberately doing something to gaslight Michael."

She winced at that. "I would hope not," she muttered. "Page can be likable when he wants to be, but you're right. He isn't the most enterprising young man."

"He's not working. He's just sitting there, living off his uncle, but why? And, if he's planning on leaving with Mel, what is he leaving with? Does the uncle have any money for him to take?"

"Okay, I really don't like all those questions," she muttered. Just then the door opened in front of them. Bethany turned and smiled. "Hey, Kassie. Is Mel here?"

"Sure, come on in."

When the woman looked curiously at the stranger beside Bethany, Conall just smiled and didn't say anything, waiting to see what Bethany would do. She was quick to introduce him. "He's here about the War Dog."

"Oh my, how much interest could there possibly be over a dog?" she asked, with a headshake.

"Have you seen him?" he asked her immediately.

She frowned. "Not recently, no, but we used to see him all the time."

"When was that?" he asked her immediately.

Kassie frowned, then looked from him to Bethany. She didn't like all the questions. "Is there a problem?"

"For one, … the *War Dog* is missing, so, yes, there's a problem," he stated, careful to keep his voice modulated and pleasant, "so we're just trying to find Bacchus, for his own sake. I hope you can understand that."

"I haven't seen him in a few days, that's for sure."

"A few days?" he repeated. The dog had been missing for a couple weeks now, so seeing him just a few days ago would be a lead.

"Maybe a little longer than that. I don't really know. Come on in," she said, as she looked over at Bethany. "I'm sure you want to talk to her about it."

"I do," Bethany replied casually.

Just then Mel came down the stairs, talking on her phone, and it was obvious she was talking to Page on Speakerphone.

"I don't know, but the guy was kind of scary at the office."

"What did you tell him?"

And then she stopped in her tracks on the stairs and said, "I've got to go," and ended the call. Her gaze went from

Bethany to Conall. "Oh."

"Yeah, *oh* is right," Bethany replied. "We need to have a talk."

Mel winced. "I don't want to talk at all."

"Really? I don't see that we have a choice."

"Is there a problem?" Kassie repeated. "Have you done something wrong, Mel?" she asked, turning to look at her daughter.

"No, Mom, of course not. I haven't done anything wrong." Then she frowned. "I mean, ... it wasn't on purpose."

Kassie stared at her in shock. "Oh, no, no, no." She went into overdrive. "If it's that damn boyfriend of yours ..."

"It's not him," Mel snapped, "and you don't know anything about it. You've got no right to judge him." She glared over at Bethany now. "I'm off shift, and these are not my work hours."

"That's true," Bethany agreed. "You are off work. However, if I find out you lied to me, ... you may not have a job to come back to," she stated.

At that, Mel's face blanched. "I didn't mean to lie." She raised both hands. "Why the hell does anybody care about a damn dog anyway?"

"Don't even go there. You work at an animal clinic. If you don't care for animals, you need to find another job. But first, you've got some explaining to do," Bethany stated. "One, for lying to your boss in the first place. Two, what happened with all that chaos at the time you were supposed to be looking after that dog? And, three, what do you know about the dog? A lot of issues are at stake here right now. So I suggest you tell us exactly what happened, and this time you better tell the truth, ... all of it."

Mel glared at her. "I'm not on the clock."

Her mom went ballistic hearing that. "Oh, no, you don't get to pull that card, when you've clearly done something wrong. You get paid when you are doing something. You don't get paid when you're sitting here having to fess up, and, girl, don't even get me started on the lying."

Someone stomped into the house behind them, and Mel's shoulders collapsed downward. "Oh, *great*," she muttered, turning to glare at her mother. "Now you've done it."

"No, I haven't. *You* have," her mom declared. "You don't get to blame others for your mistakes. Now you need to tell us exactly what's going on here."

At that, a burly man walked in, glaring at them. "What the hell is going on here?" He turned and looked at his daughter. "What am I hearing now? … What's this about you lying about something?"

She glared at her father. "Fine," she said, stomping her feet, "I didn't mean to lie. It just wasn't a big deal."

"We'll be the judge of that," Bethany stated.

"What have you done?" her father asked, glaring at Mel.

Mel, ever more defiant, replied, "I didn't do anything wrong, and you've got no reason to judge me or Page."

"Page?" her father repeated, with a deadly quiet voice.

Conall immediately stepped forward but didn't say anything.

"That's Michael's nephew," Bethany explained to Mel's dad.

Kassie's gaze went from one to the other and nodded slowly. "Yes, but we need to know exactly what's going on here," she stated, turning to look at her daughter. "Out with it. What have you done?"

"I didn't do anything. … So what? I covered up something, that's all."

"That doesn't sound like nothing. Covered up what?" her father asked, gritting his teeth.

She winced. "Everything kind of went chaotic there at the clinic because …" she explained, almost in tears, then she stopped.

"Because why?" Bethany asked.

Even Conall heard the tone of her voice and the worry in it. He reached out a hand and gripped her shoulder. "How about we just get to the truth before anybody makes this into a bigger deal than it is?"

"Says you," Kassie replied in exasperation, looking at him resentfully. "You're the one who caused all the trouble."

"I caused all the trouble?" he asked in astonishment. "By doing my job? I came here looking for Bacchus, not just any dog, but a War Dog, last seen at the clinic. Your daughter told me that she somehow lost track of it when the door was open and multiple people came and went, and she had no idea who took the dog. That was after her original story to Bethany here wasn't holding up."

He turned to look at Melanie now. "You didn't tell me that your boyfriend was there in the lobby at the time. You didn't tell me that you were spending all your time with him, and that's why you didn't take care of the job you were supposed to be doing."

There was silence for a moment, as Mel glared at him. "I wasn't doing anything wrong," she stated defiantly.

"Except that you know you're not allowed to have Page there at the clinic during work hours," Bethany stated angrily. "We already went over this."

"He was just there, dropping me off some lunch," she

replied. "What was I supposed to do? Besides, he needed a hand with something, and I didn't think you would care. I mean, … whatever. It was just a small amount anyway."

Bethany closed her eyes and breathed in for a moment, as Mel's father immediately stepped in. "A small amount of what?" he growled.

Mel turned and glared at him, then showed her palms. "Petty cash, that's all. He just needed a little bit of money, and there was money in the petty cash, so I let him have it," she explained. "I mean, it's no big deal to anybody."

Her father's faced turned thunderous, and her mother gasped in horror.

Bethany frowned, looking from one person to the next. "So, you created a commotion by letting the cat out of the cage, knowing full well the dogs in the lobby would get overexcited, and things would get chaotic in a hurry, allowing you access to steal the petty cash, while everyone was too busy to notice. In the meantime, Bacchus disappeared, so you and your boyfriend concocted all this BS about a note and saying somebody else was supposed to pick up the War Dog to explain the missing dog?"

"So, you have no idea who took the dog?" Conall was frustrated more than anything else with all the lies piling up.

Mel glared at him. "See? It's nothing, and, besides, it's just a dog. Like what is everybody freaking out about?"

"Oh, Mel," Kassie whispered, "you have no idea what you've done."

"I didn't do anything," she declared in a huff. "He just needed a few bucks, and I had to get to the petty cash and not have anybody see, so whatever," she said, with a snort. "Besides, it's back to the same old thing. … This isn't work hours, and you don't have any right to come to my house and hassle me about it."

Her father stared at her, as if he had never seen her before. He turned his gaze to his wife, Kassie.

She held up her hands and shook her head at him. "Don't say it. I'll handle it."

"You better. … I'm about done, and Mel's out."

"What do you mean, *out?*" Mel wailed, becoming the plaintive daughter. "Why would you kick me out?"

"The fact that you don't even know what you've done *is* a problem," Bethany stated, with real sadness in her voice. She was hurt, and her expression showed it.

"What? It was only like fifty bucks. … I mean, he needed the money. What do you want from me?"

"I wanted honesty," Bethany replied, with sorrow and a hint of anger in her tone, "and I wanted loyalty, integrity. I was really hoping for the truth, but apparently I didn't deserve any of those things, yet Page did. You stole from me. You lied to me. You deliberately created a situation where the animals in my care could have been hurt, losing one in the process, thus damaging my business and my reputation. All for the boyfriend. That's what the problem is."

"No, no, I didn't. It was petty cash, like for small things that we needed around the office."

"How do you figure that giving it to your boyfriend made any sense?"

"He needed it," she repeated, with a shrug.

"Oh, Lord," Kassie whispered, and it sounded more like a prayer than anything.

"I'm not even addressing all the details of this conversation," Conall stated, shaking his head, "because obviously an awful lot more here has to be worked out, but let's bring it back to Bacchus."

"Again, with the freaking—"

Conall held up his hand, before he spoke, and that shut up Mel for good. "Be careful what you say about him, young lady. That dog knows more about loyalty and honor than you ever will. So, you lied about the dog, and you lied about the note. Did you just write that out or what?"

She nodded. "Yeah, I just wrote it up, so we had an excuse for the dog disappearing. What was I supposed to say? *I let my boyfriend have the petty cash, and, in the process, the dog ran away?* Yeah, like that would do me any good."

He stared at her. "How much good is any of it doing you right now?"

Her father snorted at that and turned and walked away. "I told you," he called back. "I'm not doing this anymore. She doesn't even have a clue."

The mother groaned. "Oh my God, Mel, what you've done is bad enough, but to keep trying to justify it somehow is really ridiculous."

"Why? What's the big deal here? You're always so damn perfect. Don't you ever do anything just because you want to?"

"Are you talking about stealing from me as *just because you want to?*" Bethany asked, staring at her employee, someone she had known for years and had even babysat, as if she were some stranger.

"I didn't steal from you," she stated, with a roll of her eyes. "It was just petty cash."

Conall wanted to laugh, since Mel didn't seem to understand that petty cash was money for the office and specifically company money. Bethany shook her head at Mel, then looked over at Kassie, whose eyes were closed, as if she were trying to make this nightmare go away.

Opening her eyes, she looked at Bethany through a sheen of tears. "I am so sorry."

Bethany nodded. "You and me both." She turned to Mel. "How much did you give him?"

"I don't know. … I mean, … all of it."

"All of the petty cash?" Bethany asked.

"Yeah, it was like fifty bucks."

"No, it was more than that because I had just refilled it."

"Yeah, so that's why the money was there, which is good I guess. He needed it."

Her mother started to cry at that.

Mel added, "Besides, it's not a big deal."

"The fact that it's not a big deal *to you* explains plenty," Bethany snapped. "But it is a big deal to me because not only did you lie to me, you also stole from me, so I can't trust you, which will create a huge pain from a staffing stand-point," she stated, as she groaned inwardly, thinking about what that would mean in terms of being even more short-handed.

"What are you talking about? I can earn that money back," Mel suggested.

Her mom looked at Bethany hopefully, but Bethany immediately shook her head. "Mel, I can't possibly have you back. You put your boyfriend over the animals, deliberately creating chaos, using them as a cover so you and your boyfriend could steal from me, and *then* you lied to me about it all."

Conall stared at the tableau in front of them. "I know this is really not what anybody wants to talk about right now," he reminded everyone, "but I'm still looking for a War Dog that was negligently released from your office, and that's a whole different story than just stealing. I'm not trying to minimize the damage that was already done to the business," he acknowledged, looking from Bethany to Melanie and back, "because that is obviously pretty major as well."

"It's more major than you think," Kassie stated, turning to Mel. "You know your father won't let this one go."

"So what will he do? Ground me?" Mel whined.

Bethany turned to her and asked, "You didn't deliberately release the dog, did you?"

"No." She shrugged. "I had to open the door several times, and I saw him go out, but it's not like it was a big deal. He hangs around everyone anyway. You know it yourself, how he goes around and visits everybody."

"So, you thought it was okay to just watch a dog walk away that was still in our care, still our responsibility?"

"But my boyfriend was picking him up," she said, with an eye roll. "So it's not like it was that big of a stressor."

"Apparently nothing is a big stressor for you," Conall replied, staring at her with a headshake. "So, you have no idea where the dog went?"

"No, I have no idea where the dog went," she spat, with an exaggerated tone. She turned and looked back at her mom. "So, are you done with the interrogation now? Am I free to go?"

Kassie miserably bit her bottom lip, and Mel just turned and walked away.

Bethany called out, "You do know you're fired, right?"

Mel turned, rolled her eyes, and said, "Whatever."

"And the money you took out of petty cash will be coming out of your final paycheck."

She cried out, "That's not fair. ... He's the one who took the money. I'm not ..."

Her mother just whispered, "Oh, Melanie."

"That's so unfair," Mel cried out, staring up at Bethany. "I can't believe you would do that to me."

Bethany snorted, then shrieked in rage, "What about what you just did to me?"

"I didn't do anything to you," Mel declared, staring at her. "It was petty cash. It's not like you needed it."

"Oh my God," Kassie muttered, as she shook her head at her daughter. She stared over at Bethany. "I am so sorry."

Bethany just turned and walked out the front door. At the same time Melanie ran upstairs, crying, as if she'd been incredibly hard done by.

Conall looked over at Kassie. "From my perspective, Bethany should press charges."

"That's exactly what her father will say," Kassie muttered, tears in her eyes. "I don't even know what to do."

"As her parent, that may be a tough one to figure out, but Melanie's taken absolutely zero responsibility for any of that. I think some tough love is overdue for Melanie. If you let this slide, what else will she think she can get away with?"

"I know," Kassie whispered. "As for the dog, I really don't know where Bacchus went. … He's a beautiful dog," she whispered.

He just nodded. "One who deserves a whole lot more consideration than the entitled brat upstairs."

And, with that, he turned and walked out.

# CHAPTER 5

A S BETHANY WALKED to her vehicle, she twisted and stared back at Mel's parents' house.

"I'm sorry," Conall said at her side.

She looked at him and gave him a small smile. "I am too, in so many ways. Including the reality that tomorrow I have a full day and need somebody at the front desk, but obviously I can't have her there."

"No, you can't," he agreed, with a nod. "Mel is not the kind of person you want handling your client's animals."

"To think that she even caused the chaos to create cover for taking the petty cash and giving it to Page is unbelievable," Bethany muttered.

"And that's how we ended up losing Bacchus," he pointed out.

She agreed, not wanting to belabor the point. "I need to talk to Page—although he told me that his name was Jamie."

Conall frowned, as he pondered it all for a moment.

She shook her head. "He's been going through some name changes lately."

"As in an identity crisis or, preparing for a new identity?"

She stared at him and shrugged. "Honestly I have no clue. I don't understand what's been going on here, so I'm the last person to ask questions like that."

He nodded. Michael had also called him Page, so he

wasn't sure that Jamie was even his name. "Let's go visit Michael and see if the nephew is there. I thought the nephew was in his late twenties, early thirties?"

"He is, and that's also another reason Melanie's father is not enthused. He was initially outraged because Melanie is only twenty-two. So I'm sure he thinks the age gap is too big."

"Add in her immaturity and that gap gets even bigger. Plus the fact that Page doesn't seem inclined to work a job, and apparently they're not opposed to taking and using other people's money. That makes me a little worried about Michael, as to whether they have access to his bank account."

Her eyes widened. "Oh, good God, I sure hope not."

"I hope not too, but, if Page has access, even if he doesn't touch it now, he'll know when Michael's pension and his disability come monthly, and Page could access it anytime," Conall noted. "If Michael's not expecting any-thing, Page and Mel could wait a little bit or take little bits here and there and then clean him out."

Bethany groaned. "I would like to think that they wouldn't do that, but, after today, I think differently," she stated, hanging her head. "I'm definitely not impressed, and I'm facing a pretty rough day tomorrow because I won't have anybody to staff the front counter."

"Don't you have anybody else you could call on?"

She shook her head. "Not really. Though it's not a hard job, it does still require a certain amount of personality, tolerance, and the ability to answer the phone."

He hesitated, then offered, "Look. I can step in and an-swer the phone and move people through the office and keep things flowing. I could handle that." She stared at him in shock, and he shrugged. "I deal with animals pretty well, and

I always have," he added. "It's not as if I"—he laughed—"I can't be any worse than what you had, but maybe that's not quite correct," he said, with a smile. "Anyway, if you don't find somebody else in time, just let me know. I'm still a warm body."

She nodded, still staring at him in shock.

"I know you weren't expecting it," he said, with a shrug, "but I'm not that scary, am I?"

She chuckled. "No, you're not that scary, and the offer is very much appreciated because I honestly don't know if I can get somebody in on this short notice."

"You'll have to hire somebody else eventually."

She groaned. "The only reason I agreed to hire Mel in the first place was because I was desperate."

"Staffing is really that big of an issue here?"

She nodded. "It can be, yes, and that's frustrating in itself because we're not sure whether it's just a temporary shortage or the new wave now," she admitted, with a sigh.

"Has anybody complained about wages, or is it just the fact that they don't want to live or work here?"

"Most of them are heading for bigger towns, bigger cities," she replied, "and I can't really blame them."

"What about you? Are you okay to stay?"

"I would like to stay," she said. "I was born and raised here, and that does get in your blood."

"It does, indeed," he agreed, with a smile. "Let's go talk to Michael, make sure he knows just how vulnerable he is. I don't want to put any ideas into his head, but I don't want him to wake up one day to find he's been cleaned out because his nephew decided to go someplace better. Whatever the hell his nephew's name is, Michael better watch out."

"It would really hurt Michael if that happened."

"I know, but, if Michael has already trusted him enough to provide access to his bank account information, then it's up to Michael to make a decision, but at least it will be an informed decision."

"But even some *informed* decisions can still be made with blinders on, and that's the worst," she argued, "especially blinders where family is involved."

He smiled and nodded. "I understand, but would you feel any better if Michael ended up getting cleaned out, and we hadn't said anything?"

"No, I would feel absolutely horrible," she cried out. "I'll meet you over there."

And she got back into her car, she turned on the engine and waited for him to pull out first, then followed him, since he knew where he was going.

As he pulled up to the front of Michael's place, she watched as Page took one look at the two of them and bolted back inside, slamming the door. She groaned to herself. "Damn it, you don't have to make things harder on yourself."

But apparently he did. When they got up to the front door, nobody answered. She looked over at Conall, and he nodded. "I don't even know if Michael's here, but I can bet that the kid has been spouting off a bunch of lies in the meantime."

"Of course he'll try and save his position," Bethany murmured, as she picked up her phone and called Michael's number.

He answered in a grumpy voice. "I'm here. I'm here. What the hell is going on?"

"It's Bethany. Can we talk to you?" she asked.

"Sure, but my nephew says that I can't go to the door

and that you guys are here to cause trouble."

She sighed. "Maybe so, but it'll be trouble for him, trying to save you some trouble. Still, you need to know what's been going on."

There was silence first, then he swore softly. "I'm coming. Just give me a minute or two."

"Make sure he doesn't stop you," she murmured.

"Is it that bad?" Michael asked.

"Honestly I don't know," she admitted. "I'm not sure to what extent this tomfoolery has risen to."

Michael groaned softly. "The door shouldn't be locked, but I suspect Page has locked it because of you."

"Can you unlock it, or do we need to find another way to get in?"

"I'm in my room," he muttered. "It's a little hard for me to walk these days on my crutches, and I'm not in my chair."

"Michael, do you need help?" she asked in alarm.

He hesitated again. "I don't know. My nephew says you're here to cause trouble."

"From his perspective, I'm sure that's true, but nothing he didn't bring on himself."

"Can you give me an idea what it is?"

She looked over at Conall, who stood at her side. "His girlfriend worked for me …"

"Melanie," Michael replied, "kind of young, but a sweetheart."

"*Yeah*, … well, … she caused a ruckus at my office, so she could steal the petty cash and give it to Page, and he took off with it. That's when Bacchus got lost because they opened the door to a cat cage with dogs in the waiting room to cause enough chaos to hide their theft, when stealing the petty cash. In the meantime, the War Dog walked out the front door, and Mel couldn't be bothered to stop Bacchus. It was clearly an intentional two-person job," Bethany pointed out.

"What?" Michael asked in astonishment. "What about the animals?"

"That's the problem," Bethany replied. "The other animals were eventually contained, but Bacchus went missing because of their orchestration, and there's been no verified sign of him since."

He started swearing. "Page has been acting funny, ever since that government guy showed up, asking about the dog."

"Conall's here with me right now, and we just came from Melanie's house," Bethany shared. "So I would really like to talk to you, and I would like to talk to Page."

"I'm pretty sure he'll bolt, if I let you guys in."

"What would you like us to do?" she asked Michael, looking over at Conall. "You know this won't have a good end."

He groaned. "I was really hoping the kid had changed, that he would calm down and settle in and be a decent answer for getting me some help and some company. Yet I guess I knew. He's always been chafing at the bit, always wanting to go places, always wanting to be somebody."

"He can be somebody all he wants," she stated firmly, "but he doesn't need to do it on my dime."

"Or mine," he added heavily.

She waited and then asked, "Have you had a problem along those lines?"

"I don't know," he admitted. "I don't know."

"Then I suggest you let us in and let us help you figure it out," she suggested.

"What about this other guy, Conall? Do you trust him?"

"Yes," she confirmed, surprising herself. "I do. He's here for the well-being of the War Dog and is very unimpressed at what's going on. He's the one who brought up the fact that, if Mel and Page were willing to take money from me, we are worried about you and your money. If Mel and Page have your bank account information or anything else, then you're at risk too."

Michael started to swear. "Give me a few minutes, and I'll get to the door." With that, he ended the call.

She looked over at Conall and nodded, and he gave her a somber look. "He already had a good idea, didn't he?"

"He's aware that he could be in trouble, yes. He's not sure, but he did mention something about his money."

At that, she watched Conall's eyebrows shoot up.

"You know, the kid has probably been trying to work his way into his uncle's good graces over time, so he could have access to whatever he needed, whenever he needed it."

"I can't imagine Michael has any money worth stealing."

"No, but he gets a steady paycheck every month," Conall pointed out, "a paycheck he needs, and he can't live without it."

"Right." She winced as she thought about what would happen to Michael if he didn't get his monthly pension. "You're so right there."

"So, somebody's got to stop this punk and unfortunately his girlfriend too." He cast her a sideways glance. "I suppose you won't press charges, will you?"

She shook her head. "No, not over $75, or whatever it was. It may have been $100. Can I afford to lose it? Sure, but I'm not happy about it. I can at least withhold it from her final paycheck. More than that, I'm very unhappy about losing a staff member, putting myself back into a difficult staffing situation, but more than anything," she stated, fuming by now and looking hurt, "she put the animals at risk that were in my care, and that is unforgivable. As bad as it already is, I'm aware that it could have been so much worse."

MICHAEL FINALLY GOT the door unlocked but struggled to open it while in his wheelchair. Conall pushed it open and helped Michael get out of the way, and the two of them stepped inside. With a smile, Conall greeted the frail old man. "Hey, Michael. How are you doing?"

The old man shrugged. "I was doing better before you two showed up."

"But were you really?" he asked, looking at him intently. "Are you sure you aren't better off knowing the truth?"

His shoulders slumped, and he nodded. "I am, but, damn, it hurts."

Conall asked, "Is Page here now?"

Michael shook his head. "No. He took off out the back door."

"Of course," Conall muttered. "What we really need to know is just what all they've done and what they were prepared to do," Conall stated. "I'm not accusing anybody of anything, but I don't want to see you end up losing your pension because these two have found a way to take it out the minute it arrives."

Michael stared at them and winced. "I don't even know what I would do if that were the case," he replied bitterly. "I barely have enough to live on now. He's always asking for things I don't have, … food that I can't afford. He always wants to go downtown and pick up extras and treats. Plus he's a young man, wanting to go do things."

"He can go and do things all he wants," Conall noted, his tone hard, "but he needs to pay for it himself, and, in order to do that, he needs to get a job."

"Yeah, but then I lose him," Michael said, "and I get that, for you, it's probably not major."

Conall immediately held up his hands. "You don't know anything about me, so you can't make that judgment," he declared soberly. "I do understand, but I also see a lot of our older and disabled veterans getting abused or taken advantage of, often by family, and, I hate it. I get that some person's company is better than no company at all, but somebody you can't trust isn't a good answer."

Michael's face twisted, as he nodded. "When I was in the military," he shared, "it's all fine and dandy, and I was part of a big family. But, now that I'm not in the military anymore, everybody forgets. Sure, I might be lucky enough to have a few friends still in contact with me, but, over time, everybody forgets. Nobody cares, and none of it is important anymore." He was gulping now. "And that's—"

"Hard?" Conall filled in.

"Yeah, it is hard, and I don't like it. I never did like anything about it, and to think that now I'm stuck in that loneliness and heading down into more of it is even worse." He looked around at his house. "This is all I've got."

"Yes, and it's worth fighting for," Conall declared. "You can't allow Page to strip it all away from you."

"No, I can't," he agreed. "There'll be no food for me, and, if I ever get Bacchus back, there won't be food for him either."

Conall nodded. "Your nephew ..."

"What?" Michael asked, staring at him shrewdly. "You might as well go on and say it."

"I don't have any easy way to say this," Conall began, "but it doesn't seem like he's too brilliant."

At that, the old man snorted. "No, he isn't, and neither is that girlfriend of his. I was worried about the two of them together because they complement each other, but not in a good way."

At that, Conall nodded. "I'm sorry about that too. Her family isn't impressed with the situation right now either."

He raised an eyebrow. "Oh, I have no doubt her father is absolutely hopping mad over it. He's got no truck with lying and cheating at the best of times, but to think Melanie stole money from her work to give to Page? Well, that'll send Mel's father over the edge."

"It may already have," Bethany replied, as she looked down at him. "I don't know what Mel was thinking."

"She wasn't thinking," Michael replied. "She was just reacting. Somebody who she thinks loves her wanted something, and she was more than willing to do anything she could to keep him."

"It's a little more than that, I think," Conall added. "You're probably right to a certain extent, and young girls are very impressionable. They get a boyfriend and want to keep that boyfriend, but it is troublesome that she didn't seem to think anything was wrong with taking the money. And she's pretty upset that her paycheck will get tapped in order to recoup the money because, as far as she's concerned, your nephew should pay for it."

"Sure, he should, but you also know that he won't. Come on. Come on in," he said, as he slowly wheeled his way into the living room. "I'm not sure what I'm supposed to do now though."

"One is to change the password for all your banking," Conall stated bluntly.

Michael admitted, "I don't know how to do that."

"Do you have a laptop? Do you do online banking?"

He nodded. "Yeah, but my nephew's been doing it for me."

When Conall winced at that, Michael groaned. "You really think he'll strip me of my money?"

Conall nodded. "Right now Page is scared because we figured out what he and Mel were up to. Page doesn't want to get caught, and, with me here, … chances are Page is thinking I'll be some bad guy, who brings it all down on him, instead of seeing the reality that Page brought it all on himself." Conall shrugged. "You know what young men are like."

"Yeah, it's been a long time though," Michael muttered, "and I didn't think my nephew would be like that."

"If you have a laptop and a password," Conall said, "we can confirm that your bank balance is somewhere around what you think you should have and maybe set up an alert—in case any money is taken out that you didn't authorize."

"I had to go to the bank to authorize him to take out money as it is," Michael shared.

Conall frowned at him and then glanced at Bethany.

She was chewing her bottom lip. "Not a good sign."

"You think that's a bad idea, don't you?" Michael asked Bethany.

She nodded. "I suspect that, if he hasn't left town already, he's headed to the bank right now."

"I really can't afford to lose all my money." Michael started to fret.

Conall immediately pulled out his phone and asked for the bank name. He quickly brought up the contact information and was on the phone within minutes. When he finally got through to a bank manager, he put it on Speakerphone and had Michael identify himself.

"Hey, Michael. What's the matter?" the manager asked. "Your nephew is in here right now, getting what you needed. Did you need more?"

"No," Michael said. "I need you to stop him from getting whatever he's taking. I didn't authorize it."

Silence came on the other end. "You know you gave him access, right?"

"I gave him access so that he could help with paying the bills, but I never wanted him taking money like it's his," he replied in outrage.

"I don't know about that, but you gave him access, which means he can take out money," the bank manager explained. "I'm kind of helpless to stop him."

"And yet," Conall broke in, "if you thought there was an elder abuse situation happening right now, then surely you would do something about it."

"Sure, but I know Michael signed to let him onto the account, which means Page has every right to take out money. If you want that stopped, I need you to come down here and do something about it."

"He'll be there in ten minutes," Conall snapped, "but, in the meantime, you need to understand that a fraud is happening right under your nose and that Michael is notifying you of that right now. You are on notice. Hear it well that Page is actively defrauding Michael. His nephew is not allowed to take any money out of Michael's account as of right now, not until we get to the bottom of this."

"Who are you, and who are you to tell me anything? Until I have Michael here telling me himself, I won't listen to anybody else." Conall looked over at Michael and saw he was starting to get angry.

"Damn it, Stephen. You know me."

"Yeah, I do know you, and I also know you asked me to put your nephew on your account, which gave him access to your money."

"That was before I just found out that my nephew has been involved in stealing from the vet clinic," he bellowed. "It sounds like he and his girlfriend are getting ready to make a run for it, and, if he's there getting money out right now, I did not authorize it."

"You don't need to authorize it because he's already allowed to come here, to get money to pay bills, and to take out a certain amount of money because he needs to go get groceries."

Conall added, "Well, maybe you should find out how much money he's taking out right now and understand that, if you don't stop this, and Page does take out any money today, it will be on you, and you can bet the war department will be out to do an investigation of any abuse of our veterans."

"Hey, hey now, what? Now just hang on a minute here …"

"No," Conall snapped. "I don't know the full impact of what's going on here," he stated through gritted teeth, "but believe me that I will get to the bottom of the matter. If you are notified of a fraud in progress, and you don't do anything to stop it, the onus is on you, and you are liable for all the funds removed from that account, so you better go stop it." With that, he disconnected the call. "Let's go."

Michael had already wheeled himself to the door, but his hands were shaking. "I can't believe he would do that," He shook his head.

"Who? Your nephew?"

"No, Stephen, … the banker," he cried out.

"That's what happens when you hand over access to bank accounts to friends and family."

"Yes, but Stephen told me that Page would only be allowed to take out a reasonable amount."

"Maybe that's what he's been doing. Maybe he's been taking out a reasonable amount all along. When we get there, we'll find out how much and how often he's been withdrawing money."

It took a little bit of effort, but he managed to get Michael into his truck and got the wheelchair tucked into the bed in the back. He turned to look at Bethany.

She was already getting into her car, and she called out, "I'll meet you down there."

He nodded and headed to the driver's side. As he got in, Michael noted, "You sure got involved pretty quick."

"Yeah, well, I can't stand injustice."

"I don't want to say this place is corrupt as hell, but—"

"It's corrupt as hell?" Conall suggested.

"Yeah."

"I already saw Jake and the rest of those punk-ass kids shaking down the café for free coffee," Conall shared with a grimace, as he glanced at Michael. "So, the fact that nothing's being done about that already had me on full notice."

"And will anybody listen to you about those bullies and now my bank account?" Michael asked shrewdly.

He chuckled. "That's a good question, but I can raise a fair amount of hell. Plus I have a lot of people in my corner who don't like injustice either, especially when it comes to our veterans."

After a five-minute trip to the bank, when they got inside, the bank manager was yelling at somebody at the counter.

"I'm pretty sure we're about to find out that your account has just been emptied," Conall told Michael.

He paled. "Oh God, please not, please not."

The manager turned and now glared at Michael. "You gave him access to your account," he roared, "and we're not liable if he cleans it out."

"You told me that he'd only take a certain amount of money, for necessities only. You told me that," Michael roared back in fury. "Now you better make sure he didn't take all that money."

"He did take all of it," the bank teller interjected. "I did ask him why he was taking so much, but he flat-out told me that it was none of my business."

"Of course he did, and you gave it to him in cash, didn't you?" Conall asked, staring at them.

Michael groaned. "Even though you knew perfectly well that Page was just ripping me off? Thanks a lot for that, Stephen. Some friend you are. And you too, Henrietta."

She flushed bright red and turned to look at the bank manager. "I went to Stephen, and he told me to give Page the money."

"Was that before or after Stephen got off the phone call with us?" Conall asked.

"After."

Conall faced Stephen. "So, now we will open a formal complaint against the bank, and we will do our best to try and shut you down. The rest of you guys might as well start looking for new jobs, unless of course you are part of the fraud Stephen just perpetuated. In which case, you'll go to jail alongside your boss here."

Henrietta and the other staff stared in horror, as they heard this.

Conall shook his head. "We called Stephen to let him know that Michael's nephew was coming here to strip out the account, and he not only chose not to stop it, he personally approved it."

"I went to him and told him that it was an unusually large amount, far more than Michael ever intended, and Stephen told me that because Michael had signed our authorization and had given permission for Page to access money from the account, the amount didn't matter, and we *had* to give him the amount requested."

"I see, and what about the fact that Michael was reassured that there would be safeguards in place, and that his nephew wouldn't do this?" Conall asked the teller.

She flushed. "That is why," she replied painfully, "I went and checked with the manager." She turned and looked at Stephen. "And you know that."

He glared at her. "You don't get to throw me to the wolves because you're the one who handed out the money. You know the safeguards too."

Astonishment flashed on Henrietta's face. "Now you're blaming me?" she asked in disbelief, and thankfully a voice of reason was introduced into the chaos, as Bethany spoke up.

"First off, how much money is left? Does Michael have enough to live on for the next month, until he gets his pension? Or did you manage to hand over absolutely everything he's spent his lifetime earning? Just how much money did you give the kid, and how long ago did he leave?"

She turned to look at Conall. "We need to contact the sheriff."

"To stress my point," Stephen sputtered, "Page was listed on the account, so he had every right to take the money out of the bank, and it's not theft."

"It absolutely is theft," Conall countered, turning to look at him. "You were specifically notified of the fraudulent withdrawal attempt, and you not only chose *not* to stop the transaction, you directed an employee to complete it. Also safeguards were in place that should have prevented it, safeguards you made sure you didn't enforce. So, the real question I have is this. … How much of that money were you getting as a kickback?"

He flushed. "I wasn't getting any of it."

"*Right*, as if anybody will believe that." He pulled out his phone and immediately started texting like mad to Badger, updating him.

When Badger phoned, he roared into Conall's ear, "Are you serious?"

"Yes, I'm serious." He eyed Stephen. "The bank manager let the nephew strip Michael's account, knowing full well it was against his wishes," he stated in frustration. "Stephen, the manager, had been informed over the phone by Michael, yet refused Michael's request, saying Page had every right to that money. Yet even after that, while we were on the way here with Michael, the bank teller went to the manager to state that the nephew wanted to withdraw an unusually large amount and asked if she should contact Michael about it—which of course she should have, without even needing to ask."

As his voice carried throughout the bank, the teller, Henrietta, flushed. "Excuse me, I know you are on the phone, but I want you to know that the last time I did do that," she explained, "*I'm* the one who got in trouble."

"Now you're in trouble again," Stephen, the manager, declared, with a sneer, "because you're the one who let Page have the money."

"On your say so," Henrietta replied, almost in tears.

Badger was still in the background on the phone, listening to the finger-pointing. "They're really a lovely outfit, aren't they?"

"It's awful when small community banks are making money off the backs of common folks. I wouldn't be at all surprised if Stephen didn't take a kickback from this."

Michael shook his head. "I didn't have enough money for there to be a kickback," he stated sorrowfully, "but I need that money to put food on the table and to pay my utility bills, which …" Michael asked in a panic, "Did he … Did Page pay the property taxes last week?"

Henrietta looked at him and slowly shook her head. "I asked him about that, and he told me that you would pay online."

He stared at her. "Oh my God, no. So you let him take the money for my property taxes too?"

She turned and looked at her boss. "You see? That's what happens when you abuse people like this."

"Not me," Stephen argued, then turned and sneered at Michael. "We told you that your nephew would have complete access."

"You also assured me that he would only be allowed to withdraw money that was reasonable and fair."

"You trusted the wrong person," Stephen stated, with a shrug, as he turned and walked back to his office. He added, "If you're thinking about causing any kind of trouble, don't bother. It won't do you any good." And, with that, he went inside his office and slammed the door.

Into the phone, Conall asked Badger, "Did you hear that?"

"Oh, I heard it," Badger replied, his tone turning lethal. "We'll see about that." Badger could be heard clicking on his keyboard.

"A few other hoods are working in this town unchecked," Conall shared, "so I'm guessing Stephen's counting on the local authorities to back him up, just leaving Michael here to twist in the wind."

"Of course, and what's Michael supposed to do for dinner tonight?" Badger asked.

"I would say, absolutely nothing, except for what he's got at home."

Michael shook his head. "I ain't got nothing at home, nothing. Page was supposed to go shopping, and I've been bugging him to go for a couple days, but he didn't."

"*Right,*" Bethany muttered, rubbing her face.

Conall frowned at her. "Maybe Page didn't pick up his girlfriend, so that he wouldn't have to share the money," Conall suggested.

She nodded, then asked Michael, "What about your car? Did you give that to him?"

"No, I didn't give it to him," Michael replied, hanging his head. "There was always hope that maybe one day I could get the vehicle adapted, so I could drive again." At this point, he was beyond himself in grief. "But he has been using it, so I suppose he'll say that, just because he's been using it, it's his."

Conall added, "He can say what he wants. If it's not his, now it's stolen because you didn't give him permission to take the money and run, did you?" Conall asked Michael.

"No, I told him to go for the groceries that we needed."

"Right," Conall said, speaking into the phone again. "Did you hear that?"

Badger replied, "Yeah, give me the license plate numbers on it."

Conall quickly gave Badger the information, as Michael passed it on. "I don't suppose you have any idea which direction he's going?" Conall asked Michael.

Henrietta, the teller, spoke up. "He was talking about California."

"Of course he was," Conall muttered.

Badger said, "I'm on it," and he quickly disconnected.

Henrietta looked over at Conall. "Does that mean you've got pull that you can use to help Michael? Honest to God, Michael, I swear I went and asked my boss, but he told me that I had to give Page the money."

Michael stared at her. "You also know that you didn't have to do what Stephen said. And that, even if you had given Page any sort of push back, he would have backed down," he muttered, glaring at her.

She flushed and shook her head. "I wondered about that, but Page's been different the last few times he's been in. He's become a little more arrogant, a little more … cocky somehow, definitely not nice."

"Of course not," Michael muttered, pulling on his chin. "He was making plans." Michael shook his head. "Print me off a statement, showing how much money he took and how much I have left."

She hesitated.

"What?" He glared at her. "Give it to me straight. I don't have time or patience for any games right now."

"Nothing's left, Michael. Page took everything out of the account."

If there was ever a moment that Conall could see a man wanting desperately to cry, yet holding it back, this was it. He put his hand on Michael's shoulder. "We'll get him."

"I don't really want to punish him," he whispered, looking up at Conall, "but I surely could use those few dollars back."

"Yeah, you sure could," Conall agreed, "but I mean it. We'll get him."

Henrietta said, "Let me print off the statement for you, so you have the numbers down."

Conall added, "You should also know that Page and Mel have also stolen from the veterinary clinic too."

Her gaze widened as she stared at Bethany, who just nodded.

"Not a large amount of money," Bethany clarified, "but between him and Melanie, they ended up emptying out the petty cash. They caused a disturbance as a cover, which is how Michael's War Dog went missing. Once Page got that money from my clinic, he apparently proceeded to implement his plan to leave and obviously cleaned out Michael's accounts on his way out of town," she explained.

Henrietta moaned. "Good God, it's really such a small amount of money to have done something like that."

"But sadly, in this case, that *small amount of money* is everything for Michael," Bethany stated, "which you know all too well."

Ashamed and upset, Henrietta headed over to her teller station and proceeded to click away on the keyboard. As soon as she was done, she brought a printout to Michael. "Here you go."

He looked down at it, expecting what he might see, yet it was still a shock for it to be there in black and white. When the tears slowly formed on his cheeks, Conall again placed a hand on his shoulder.

"You'll be okay."

Michael shook his head. "How will I ever be okay again?" he muttered.

"For one thing, we need to take Page's name and access off the account. That way, when your pension deposit drops in again, Page can't continuously take more money." Conall looked over at Henrietta, with a stern expression. "How was it set up? Because we need to get that stopped too."

She winced. "I don't know that I can do that without Page's signature."

"In that case," Bethany stated, "we need to open a new account right now, and we need to call and get the deposit changed to ensure the money goes into the correct account."

Henrietta brightened at that. "Now that I'm sure you can do." She raced back over, and it took a little bit to open another account.

Conall looked over at Bethany, as she continued to stay with them. "Are you sure you want to stay?"

"Yeah, I'm in for the long haul," she stated grimly. "I didn't think Page and Mel were that smart."

"Yeah," Conall replied, "that's about how I feel right now too. I thought he wasn't too smart, but he knows the pension goes into this account every month, and he didn't have to do much to access it either. He can just steal and keep on moving."

"Then what?" Michael asked, staring at them. "That's no way to live, and he's hardly thirty yet."

"Yeah, but, at the rate he's going, … he won't make it

much past thirty either."

Michael nodded slowly. "You're right. He'll get in trouble, won't he?"

"Yeah, he sure will. The money won't keep him very long, and, for all we know, he needed this money for something else too."

"Do you know if he has any friends?" Bethany asked Michael.

"Just that set of rotten ones, Jake and his merry band."

"Of course Page would be connected to the punks in town," Conall said, with a groan. By the time they were finished at the bank, with a new account set up, Conall had already texted Badger the routing and new account numbers so that Kat could deal with it. "Now *that* I can really get behind. Kat has some major connections."

Michael asked, "Who is Kat? What does Kat do, and who calls herself Kat anyway?"

Conall chuckled. "She's a specialist in prosthetics, and she works with the Veteran's Department a lot. So, if anybody can get us to the right people to confirm that your pension deposit gets changed to your new account right now, it's her. We'll also see if we can get a lawyer for you."

"For what?" Michael asked.

"To get the money that Page stole back from the bank," Conall replied, with a smile. "I doubt your nephew will have very much of the cash still on him, but he'll learn very, very quickly that the amount of money he took doesn't go very far. Not to mention we need to file a stolen vehicle report."

"A damn sad day," Michael noted, with a nod, "when your own kin steals from you."

"An even sadder day when your bank doesn't do anything to stop it, when you are asking them to do just that,"

Bethany stated loudly, glaring at Henrietta.

Henrietta looked at her and nodded. "But you must understand that I'm also limited by what I can do. Michael did sign to allow his nephew to have access."

"Of course I did," Michael wailed. "I'm in a damn wheelchair. What else am I supposed to do?"

She winced and nodded. "I know. I understand that, and, in most cases, it would have been fine."

"But not in this case because of Page, is that what you mean?" Conall asked.

She nodded. "That's exactly what I mean. We haven't seen a case like this in a long time, but it does happen."

"It shouldn't," Michael stated bitterly. "Family is supposed to be there for each other."

"All too often, they rip off each other instead," Henrietta conceded, "and I'm sorry for my part in it. I'm doing everything I can to help you right now, but I don't know what else I can do."

Michael muttered to himself, sinking into his chair.

Bethany looked over at Henrietta and nodded. "I don't know how this will come out, but make sure that you do everything you can. Otherwise it'll come back on you."

She nodded. "I did get permission from the manager before I released the funds," she reiterated. "I wasn't happy about doing that, but Stephen told me that we had absolutely no other way to handle it because Michael had already signed the documents."

"So, there are no checks and balances, despite what Michael was told by Stephen?" Conall asked. "Especially if you know that somebody is up to no good, setting out to steal from another person, yet you complete the transaction anyway?"

Henrietta shrugged. "It depends on the bank's policies," she murmured, "and, yeah, in case you're wondering, this is my last day."

"Was it intended to be your last day?" Conall asked.

"No," she replied, with a sheen of tears in her eyes, "but I don't need any more of this or of *him*," she shared, tossing a glance toward the closed office door.

"It's probably just as well, and you'll be even better for these mitigating actions you did after the theft, but it won't stop you from being part of the investigation," Conall warned her.

She winced and nodded. "I figured as much. That's the way it works, right?"

Conall gave her a crooked smile. "So hold tight, tell the truth, and see how you fare in the end."

"I didn't do anything," she snapped, glaring at him.

"No, except that you did give Page the money. Yeah, I get it. You asked Stephen if that was a thing you had to do, and your boss said yes, which was unfortunate, but you still might have to testify."

"It's not a huge amount of money though."

At that, Michael started to huff and puff. "Maybe not to you," he yelled, staring at her in shock, "but that's my food, my utilities, my property taxes. I can't just walk to a shop and get something anytime I want, you know?" he said, fuming. "Not in a wheelchair and not without any money."

"Which is also why we'll get your money back," Bethany murmured.

Michael looked at her, but even Conall could see his rheumy eyes tear up, as he shrugged. "That's one part of the pain," he muttered. "The other part? Well, that'll take longer to get over."

That was hard because there was no way to misunderstand what he meant. Betrayal by family was one of the worst things that could happen.

Unfortunately it was also one of the most common.

# CHAPTER 6

BETHANY DROVE BACK to Michael's place, her heart throbbing with sadness. Both she and Michael had been ripped off, but one was much more devastating than the other. When she checked out her pockets, she found some cash on her. As they went back in Michael's house, she got in just ahead of them and wandered into the kitchen to see what he had for food, then winced because there was really nothing. Not even milk for a cup of tea. As soon as the men got inside, she looked over at Michael and asked, "Did you give Page a grocery list?"

He nodded. "Yeah, and it was pretty long too because I'd been fighting to get him to go shopping, as we're down to nothing," he said sadly.

"Any chance that you have a copy of the list lying around?"

"I don't have a copy, and who knows what he did with it." Michael eyed her shrewdly. "Why?"

"I'll go get you some groceries, but I don't know what you want."

He shook his head. "I don't need charity."

She snorted. "It's hardly charity," she argued, "and we all need help at some point in time. I don't even have a receptionist for tomorrow now because mine was too busy stealing for her boyfriend to do her job," she added, with an eye roll.

His shoulders slumped and in a formal voice he replied, a bit too low, "I won't accept charity, but, if you could possibly lend me a little bit of money, … I would be very grateful."

She nodded. "We can do it that way, if you want," she murmured, "but I still need to know what to get you."

He frowned, as he looked around. "I really need coffee. I didn't get any today."

She stared at him intently. "What kind of coffee would you want?"

He shrugged. "Whatever is cheapest honestly. That's all I can afford."

She winced, realizing just how rough things were looking for him. Then she sat down with a piece of paper that she snagged from the coffee table. "Okay, let's go through some of the groceries you'll need."

By the time she got that done, she hopped up and turned to the front door. "I'll head out now, get you all this stuff, and then we'll go from there."

He sighed. "You don't have to do this, you know?"

She looked over at him and smiled. "I don't *have* to do anything," she stressed, "but sometimes it's good to do something nice for someone. I'm not impressed with what's happening in my corner of the world either, but it makes me happy to help you."

With that, she stepped outside. As she went to close the door behind her, Conall was there and shoved a couple hundred dollar bills in her hand.

"Use this." She looked at it, frowning, and he shook his head. "Don't even start with me, or I'll give you the same argument you just gave Michael."

She groaned. "I can cover it, you know?"

"I know," he replied, studying her. "Believe me that there isn't a veteran out there I wouldn't help if I could."

Such anger and sincerity filled his tone that she nodded, realizing that this had hit Conall hard too and on a level that she couldn't even assess or understand. She didn't have any experience with military, active or ex, and to think that this brotherhood would help Michael perked her up.

"Is there any way you can help him?" she whispered.

"Working on it," he muttered. "I'm not sure what our options are yet, though." He sighed. "Go ahead and get the groceries."

She nodded and hopped into her vehicle. It took her a good forty minutes at the grocery store to sort through the few things that he relayed to her and to add some other things she thought he could use. She texted him several questions, and. by the time she had a hefty load bought and paid for and was loading it into her car, time had really raced by. When she pulled into Michael's driveway, Conall came out and helped her unload.

"I went through the cupboards and started a spaghetti sauce of sorts," he shared, "but Michael could really use a cup of coffee, and he was wishing he'd put cookies on the list."

She chuckled. "I did pick up some cookies, so I'm hoping he'll be okay with my choice."

He smiled. "That was one thing about my granddad. He ate very healthy most of the time, but, damn, he wanted his cookies."

She laughed, loving that. "I think that, given what they've been through, if they want a cookie, they should be allowed a damn cookie."

"Agreed."

Once inside, she sniffed the air. "Wow, are you telling me that you cook too?"

"Not only does he cook," Michael perked up, wheeling into the kitchen, "it smells divine." He looked back at him. "You need a place to stay by any chance?"

Conall looked over at him. "I'm staying at the motel, … but I could stay here if you would rather." He thought about it and then shrugged, looking from one to the other. "That's not a bad idea."

As she thought about it, she nodded. "It is a great idea because that nephew of his is bound to come back."

"He won't hurt me though," the old man declared immediately. "I know that."

She turned to Michael and smiled. "He may not want to hurt you or may not think he will, but he's already inflicted great pain. So I don't know where in his mind that hurt stops and starts."

The words hit the old man like a blow, and he sucked in his breath, slowly nodding. "You do pack a punch sometimes, girl."

She looked over at Conall, who was on the phone with his motel and very quickly had things arranged. Disconnecting, he told Michael, "It's all good. I'll be your roommate for a few days."

Michael smiled. "I don't suppose you want to hear a couple war stories, do you?"

"Hey, I've got some of my own to tell too," he stated, with a grin.

Michael caught the expression on Bethany's face. "Don't worry," he told her. "We'll be fine."

She nodded. "I know, but honestly I was planning on taking Conall's offer to work for me tomorrow."

Conall burst out laughing. "I'm pretty sure I can do both."

"Okay, good," she said, "at least for tomorrow."

"What's this all about?" Michael asked.

She explained and Michael nodded. "Yeah, you really don't want anybody at your clinic who doesn't have the animals' interests at heart," Michael noted. "I really, really do want Bacchus back again."

"That is still something we'll have to sort out sooner rather than later," Conall agreed, shaking his head, "but first you'll have a hot meal." He asked, "What time of day do you normally sleep?"

"Well, two o'clock in the afternoon for a nap," he shared, with a snort. "For bedtime, I like to get to bed around nine. It depends on whether I catch any sleep at night or not."

"You're not sleeping either?"

He shook his head. "No, haven't slept well in a very long time."

"Of course you haven't," Conall murmured, as if that were the most normal thing in the world.

Bethany frowned. That would be something she would ask him about.

Conall turned to her and added, "I made enough spaghetti for you too."

Her eyebrows shot up, and Michael looked at her with a big smile. "It would be lovely to have company," he admitted shyly.

She immediately nodded, knowing there was no way to turn down an invitation like that. Looking over at Conall, she smiled. "It smells wonderful."

"Good, sit down," he said, with a smile. "Dinner's ready,

just let me finish putting a final touch on it," he added, as he did a taste test and then nodded. "Let's grab plates and cutlery and sit down to eat."

Together, the two of them set the table and got Michael in place, where a plate of spaghetti was put before him. He looked at it in amazement. "If you could bottle this, I could eat this way every day."

"I made enough for you to have three to four days of it," Conall stated. "However, considering I'll be here for a few days, I would suggest that we freeze these leftovers, so you'll have a few meals set aside. Then I'll cook more meals the next couple days, where we can freeze those leftovers too, while I'm here. That way, when I leave, you'll be set for a bit."

Michael frowned, seemingly perturbed. "I really don't want to be a bother."

"Oh, I know. I hear it in your voice," Conall replied, with a smile. "But I also know that my old granddad would have my head on a platter if I didn't do this for you. We veterans have to stick together. It's a tough-enough world, so we should help each other when we can." Conall smiled. "Besides, absolutely no reason not to."

"You're right there," Michael whispered, "but it does seem like a long time since anybody cared."

"That will change, starting today," Bethany interjected. "Don't you worry. We've got your back."

He looked over at her, gave her half a smile, and nodded. "Sweetheart, you can have my back anytime you want."

She burst out laughing. "And I bet you were quite the ladies' man in your day."

"What do you mean, *in my day?*" he asked with a broad smile, as he pounded his wheelchair.

And that set the tone for dinner.

As soon as Bethany left, and, with Michael in much better spirits, Conall turned to him and asked, "Now, do you want to get settled in your room, or are you okay out here? I want to go out and do some hunting for the War Dog."

"Go hunt the dog," Michael said immediately. "I'm good right here. I've been alone for a long time. I'll be just fine."

"I know you have. Sometimes being alone is good, and sometimes being alone is damn hard," Conall noted. "I do want to get out and get some idea of where that dog could have gone."

"I've got no clue," Michael muttered.

"Do you have any idea where the dog has been going during the day?" Conall asked in a casual tone. "That is most likely where he's ended up."

Michael frowned. "I didn't even think about that." He shook his head. "I should have, damn it. … I should have."

"Let's not worry about the *should haves* now. Let's just think about where Bacchus has gone because, if nobody's seen him out and about, it's possible that he may be doing just fine in his new location."

"I wonder," he muttered, waving him off.

Conall quickly walked outside, stopped at the door, and looked back at Michael. "Does your nephew have his own keys?"

Michael frowned and then nodded. "Yeah, but I never really lock my doors anyway."

"Tonight we'll lock them when we go to bed," Conall

suggested, "and we'll get the locks changed tomorrow."

Michael's shoulders slumped, as he stared at him. Then he slowly nodded. "I guess we need to, *huh?*"

"Yes, I would say so," Conall agreed. "I don't know what Page has got to say for himself, but he won't be taking any more from you."

A smile cracked Michael's face. "You won't let up on him, will you?"

"No, I sure won't," he declared. "Give me a couple hours and try to get some rest, if you can."

With that, Conall hopped into his truck and pulled out of the driveway. He wasn't even sure where to start, but heading out from the vet's clinic would be a good place.

He parked in the parking lot, wondering at his impulse to volunteer to handle her front desk tomorrow, but considering that some of this chaos was partly his fault, he felt that he needed to step in. Besides, Bethany was damn cute, and she was also the kind of person who he could appreciate.

And, for him, he believed that one good turn deserved another.

As he got out and walked around the parking lot, he got a phone call. He answered it to find Badger checking in. "Not much to say. I'm tracking right now," Conall greeted him. "So far, the only things I know are that this little town is dying, it's got way-too-many bullies, and I've been lied to one time too many already."

Badger laughed. "Keep me updated." Then he disconnected.

The next call came from Bethany.

"What are you doing in my parking lot?" she asked in exasperation.

He snorted. "I'm glad you've got cameras."

"Yes, I've got cameras, and I was just absentmindedly clicking through, trying to process everything. I wasn't even paying attention, and suddenly I see you wandering around."

"With everything else going on, I can't forget the reason I'm here."

"Bacchus," she said.

"Yeah, Bacchus."

"What will you do here?"

"I'm checking to see if there are any tracks."

"It's been weeks though," she explained.

"I know, and that's part of the problem. It's been weeks. So, the question is, … why has nobody seen him?"

There was silence on the other end at first. "Do you really think Mel knows something?"

"She won't be too willing to talk to us."

"No, she won't, especially now that her father's on the rampage and is ready to kick her out of the house."

"So she didn't leave with Page? Boy, I bet she's mad. And I'm not against her father kicking her out now too," Conall added. "Mel apparently doesn't have any life skills or a very good check on reality. How else will she get that unless somebody kicks her out on her own and sees what happens?"

Bethany sighed. "I'm sure that's exactly what'll happen to her. Unfortunately, as you saw, she's blind to what real life is like."

"I know, but we can't take on her care as well as everybody else's right now," he stated. "What I'm looking for is the War Dog."

"Do you want me to come down there and take a look?"

"Didn't you take a look already?"

"I did," she confirmed. "I immediately walked for what

seemed to be hours, calling for him, but there was just nothing. I didn't get any wind of anything, and that really concerned me. I thought at one point that something might have gotten him, but Bacchus is big and in good shape."

"Still, do you have wolf problems here?" Conall asked, turning, looking around. "That would be about the only wild animal that could take him down."

"No wolves that I know of," she murmured, "at least I hope not."

He smiled. "As far as I know there aren't. I did some research on that before I got here, but you never really know."

"Bacchus is pretty big and healthy, but he is missing a leg."

"Yes, and there is always that. It was one of the reasons that he was given to Michael in the first place, since Michael is missing a leg as well."

"Everybody loves Bacchus," she said. "It just breaks my heart to think that something happened to him."

"Something *has* happened to him. The question is whether it's bad or not." And, on that cryptic note, he added, "I'll call you back later, if I find something."

# CHAPTER 7

W HEN BETHANY GOT up the next morning, not having heard from Conall, she had to admit she was disappointed. The man seemed to make miracles happen—or at least get things started. She didn't know so much about whether he had the ability to finish what he was starting or not, but she liked what she'd seen. At first glance, he could be scary, yet he was definitely all heart, and there was nothing to *not* like about that.

She hadn't mentioned anything to him about what time she would need him at the clinic and knew that it was a huge imposition to even ask him. Yet agreeing to it probably wasn't the wisest thing for her to have done in the first place. Especially considering he didn't know the lay of the land or anything about how the office worked. Yet, as she drove in a half hour earlier this morning, she found him standing outside her clinic, talking on his phone. She hopped out and looked at him in surprise.

He shrugged, "Reporting for duty, unless you're not sure."

"Of course I'm sure," she replied, "but honestly I thought you might be too busy now."

He tilted his head. "But I promised."

"Right," she confirmed, with a gentle smile, "and that means a lot to you."

He raised an eyebrow. "Doesn't it to you?"

"Yes," she stated. "That is also why I cannot make too many promises because, when you get pulled too often, too far, it's much too hard to ensure that you do everything that you need to do. Plus sometimes the *you* part—as in the *me* part—loses out."

He looked at her for a long moment and nodded. "It's all about balance, isn't it? Sounds to me as if you haven't had a whole lot of that either."

"The ongoing staffing shortage has been pretty rough," she admitted. "I do the very best I can for the animals in my care, but I still need help—and now I've lost one more helper."

"Yeah, but *that one* you didn't need."

She unlocked the door, shut down the security system, and opened the front door, for him to walk in. "I mean, I understand if you don't want to be here."

"Stop it," he told her. "I said I would be here, and I'm here."

"Good enough," she conceded, and she hesitated for a moment. "Can you handle phones?"

He plucked his cell phone from his pocket and waggled it at her.

"I know. I know," she said, "but it's a business phone, like a landline."

"I'm not that old," he argued. "Besides, it's a phone. I can figure it out."

She flushed, realizing that she was basically worrying over nothing. "Fine, just tell everybody that we're very short-staffed and that I'll have to get back to them."

"That's fine," he said, with a nod. "Presumably you also have a schedule to follow, so I can check people in. Do you do anything with them outside of checking them in and getting them settled in the lobby, until a room is available?"

"That's pretty much it," she replied. "Obviously, if you had more training, I could put you to a lot more work."

"Ha, don't get so cheeky that you think I'm staying."

She laughed. "Are you kidding? If you're any good, I would be desperate to keep you as it is," she admitted, "but I understand it's not likely your thing."

"I don't know what my thing is anymore," he admitted, with a lazy smile in her direction.

That smile stopped her in her tracks. "You should stop using that smile." She wagged a finger at him. "That's a dangerous weapon."

He chuckled. "That's the first time I've ever heard that."

"Ha, you know you are way too cute already."

"*Ha*," he repeated, mocking her tone. "I really don't think so."

She smiled. "Anyway, we open at eight, and I do need to get the OR ready."

"Do you have somebody to help you in surgery today?" he asked.

She nodded. "As long as Liza, my vet assistant, shows up, I should be good."

Within a few minutes another woman joined them. She eyed Conall with suspicion. Then, when Bethany gave her the rundown of what had happened, her face immediately spiked with fury.

"That bitch," she snapped. "That silly little child. I've caught her picking up things from the office and just taking them home."

At that, Bethany turned and looked at her sharply. "What?"

"Yeah, just stupid stuff—a pen here and there, some paper clips—and I wondered at the time, ... was she a kleptomaniac and had a real problem? I told her to knock it off, that you still had to buy everything that was here, but she just laughed and said, '*Everybody steals from offices.*'"

"Yet she didn't need it, did she?" Bethany asked.

"No, she didn't need it," Liza declared. "I don't know that she did it again. She hasn't been here very long, but obviously ... she graduated from that to something much bigger."

"I had just topped up the petty cash too," Bethany shared. "Close to one hundred bucks was in there."

"And all for the boyfriend, all for the thrill," Conall pointed out, "particularly if she's also been busy helping herself to other things in the office. A lot of people don't consider taking office supplies as theft."

Bethany shook her head. "Yet all kinds of studies had been done about how many thousands of dollars go missing every year because of things like that. I honestly don't care about the petty cash nearly as much as I do about what she did to create the cover disturbance. Causing all that stress to the animals and our clients was so irresponsible. I'm just thankful that none were hurt."

"That was completely unacceptable," Liza agreed. "I can't even believe Mel did that."

After discussing it for a few more minutes, Bethany headed back to prepare for surgery, while Liza looked over at Conall. "How the hell did she find you?"

"I'm here searching for Bacchus, the War Dog," he replied, "and that's caused so much chaos that I offered to give her a hand, while she finds somebody."

"Good luck with that," Liza muttered, with a headshake.

"Do you have anybody in mind who may know where the dog is?" If he hadn't been watching her face, he wasn't sure he would have caught it, but almost immediately there was the briefest expression change, then she shrugged.

"I don't know about that," Liza said. "I'm kind of surprised that nobody's heard from him."

"That's the part I don't know about either," Conall replied. "The way it sounds, it's as if Bacchus roamed around town, you would think somebody would have seen him somewhere."

She nodded, then showed him around briefly. He had a five-minute tour of the place to get started. Then Liza disappeared, and Bethany popped her head in to add, "If it gets too bad, let us know."

He waved his hand and smiled. "Go on. Take care of the animals."

She smiled. "Okay, I'm about to open the front door, so it'll get crazy pretty quickly."

WHEN BETHANY SAID to expect *crazy*, she meant it. Conall was happy for her because it meant that the clinic was successful and that she was obviously a good vet and well loved. People looked at him in surprise, while manning the front desk, but he just smiled and explained that he was the temporary help. That seemed to settle them down, and, for some, it made them seem a whole lot calmer.

He'd always been good with animals, and not one that showed up gave him any trouble at all. He did ask several people about the War Dog, if they had seen him at all. Everybody just shook their heads, and most weren't even aware that Bacchus was missing.

Conall just nodded and kept on working. The copy machine was a bit of an anomaly to him, so he left that for later—when he had a chance to sort it out. Yet he got the coffeemaker down pat and in no time was rocking and rolling through his morning, and everything was going fine.

When he looked up a few hours later, Bethany stood there, her hands on her hips, staring at him. He looked at her in confusion. "So, that's kind of an angry look. Did I mess something up?"

"No," she said, her face softening. "Not angry at all. Not at you. I'm just wondering how the hell my temporary volunteer is better than the person I had hired."

He smiled. "Because you can make a big job out of nothing, or you can just take a big job and get after it," he explained. "I've always been a doer more than a talker."

"And yet look at you," she said, with a smile. "Almost everybody I've seen today has made a comment about your calming presence and how nice it was to see somebody, particularly a male somebody, behind the desk. I never knew anybody cared."

"I don't think it's a gender thing at all," he explained. "I get along with the animals, so maybe it's not as chaotic."

"And that blows me away," she muttered. "Anyway, this is your time to grab some lunch."

He sighed. "Yeah, I didn't get that far."

"Of course you didn't, but you probably made sure Michael had food, didn't you?"

He smiled. "I left him a bowl of spaghetti, all wrapped up in the fridge, ready to microwave."

Just then his phone rang, and he dealt with it very quickly. When he hung up, he said, "Sorry about that."

"Sorry for what?"

"Getting phone calls at work."

She snorted. "It's not as if you're getting paid, and this is hardly your job, but I am curious as to what that was."

"I'm getting Michael's locks changed, so the nephew can't come in and take anything else that he thinks might be worth a penny or two."

"Good Lord," she muttered, "and he would do that too."

"You might want to consider it here too, … especially if Melanie has keys."

She winced and immediately pulled out her phone and contacted Mel's mother. "Hey. I'll need the keys to the vet clinic back from Mel. Any chance you could bring them by yourself?"

"I haven't seen her all day," Kassie wailed, her tearful voice on the other end loud enough to reach Conall's ears too.

Conall winced and asked Bethany, "What are the chances she took off with Page?" His voice carried through the phone, and Kassie started to cry even harder.

Kassie groaned. "In that case, I don't know what to do about the keys."

"Could you check and see if she left them behind?" Bethany asked Kassie. Whatever the answer was, Bethany didn't like it at all. When she finally hung up, she looked over at Conall. "She doesn't know if the keys are even there, but she assured me that she will look."

"That would help," he replied. "How long has Melanie worked for you?"

"Not long, but enough to settle in a little bit," she noted, with a groan. "I really don't want the added expense of changing all the locks, but I can't take the chance of her doing something stupid either, especially if she's still with Page."

Conall nodded.

When the phone rang a few minutes later, it was Kassie, saying she found them. Turning her cell phone off and putting it away, Bethany looked at him with a bright smile. "She'll bring the keys down."

"Good, that's helpful and one less thing to worry about."

She looked at him. "Do you think we have a pair of budding thieves right now? Is this how they get started?"

"I don't know about that," he admitted, "but sometimes desperation makes people do all kinds of strange things."

"Maybe," she muttered, "it still feels very wrong. Do you think I need to change my locks?"

"You have a security system, and it's always on, right?"

"I do, and it does tell me if anybody has accessed the building."

"So, I'll keep a close eye on your security for the next little bit, just as you did finding me in your parking lot last night," he added, with a smile.

"You didn't call me back. … I was waiting to hear from you."

"There was nothing to say," he stated. "Nothing was found."

She nodded. "I didn't really expect you to find anything because I couldn't find anything either, but I was hoping for something."

He smiled at her. "Oh, I'll find Bacchus."

When Liza came out, needing Bethany's attention, the conversation ended.

He returned his attention to work but kept an eye out

for Melanie or Page or even Bacchus. Not until the end of the day did Bethany come out from the back, looking tired, her fatigue evident on her face. "I really appreciate the help today," she muttered, dropping in the chair in front of him. "It's always worse when it's a surgery day. I can generally handle the clinic if it's just appointments because I can put up a sign saying I'm short-staffed and, if I'm not out here, I'm meeting with somebody in the back. Yet I don't really like to leave the building wide open."

"Not right now especially. If you are closing up the clinic now or just don't need me at the front desk anymore, I'll head out to look for Bacchus again."

"I don't understand where you can go and where you can look," she admitted in confusion. "What can you do when nobody's seen Bacchus in weeks?"

"I don't know specifically, but I just keep at it. That's what I'll do." She just nodded. He smiled, then turned and walked away.

"You never got lunch, did you?" she called out.

"I'll get something in a couple hours when I'm done."

"Make sure to call and let me know you're okay."

He stopped, looked at her in surprise, and then nodded. "I will." With that, he turned and left.

---

# CHAPTER 8

BETHANY WATCHED, AS he walked outside, hopped into his vehicle, and drove away. She shook her head. "What could he possibly see driving around in the truck?" Yet she also knew that he must have a plan.

"Interesting person," Liza noted from behind Bethany, "and he seemed to handle the office pretty well."

She looked over at her and smiled. "He was a freaking lifesaver today. I still can't believe l asked a veteran to answer my phones."

"No, I can't either," Liza said, on a chuckle. "Still, all this mess with Mel and Page just makes me very sad." Liza watched Conall's vehicle disappear from the parking lot. "What's he doing now?" she asked.

"He'll go look for Bacchus." She noted that Liza shifted uncomfortably. Groaning softly, Bethany suggested casually, "Look. If you know anything, please say so. You have no idea how this is steamrolling potentially into something big."

Liza winced but added, "I don't know anything for sure, but I wondered if I saw Bacchus a few days ago, but I didn't know who he was with or if it was even him."

"And you didn't say anything?"

"If I would have been sure, I would have, but, … but I wasn't. Although I do know that the dog I saw was happy, so I figured it wasn't a problem anyway."

"However, it is a problem because Bacchus is a War Dog," Bethany pointed out, "and Conall is here on behalf on the War Department."

Liza immediately winced. "Oh, God, I should have mentioned that earlier to him."

"I suspect he already knows that you didn't because he mentioned something about you."

She stared at her in shock. "What do you … What do you mean?"

"He's somebody who very easily seems to know who's lying," she shared, with a shrug.

"So, what do I do now?" Liza stared out the window glumly. "I didn't set out *not* to tell him. I just didn't want to give him half answers, not when I don't really know anything."

"But even half answers are something. He could have headed in that direction and maybe checked it out. You should tell him. If it wasn't all that far from here, maybe text him to let him know." She looked over at her surgical assistant.

Liza nodded. "That's probably the best answer. Can you text him for me? I don't have his number." And Liza gave Bethany the location where she might have seen Bacchus.

Bethany quickly pulled out her phone and sent Conall a text, giving him the sketchy details, yet not naming Liza as the source.

His response came back. **Is that what Liza told you?**

Bethany held out her phone for Liza to see.

Her face paled. "His lie radar really is kind of scary."

"He is kind of scary, but he also did a hell of a job in the office," Bethany noted wistfully, as she turned and looked around.

"You're not thinking about keeping him on, are you?" Liza asked.

She snorted, staring at her assistant. "I doubt that this is even something he could take on, considering he's here on behalf of the War Department," she reminded her, "but we would be blessed to have him for any time we could get him. He handled all the people and the animals so easily."

"But we didn't exactly have anybody cranky today."

"Oh, I don't know about that. John Bennett was here, and you know that he always makes the girls cry."

Liza nodded slowly. "John is a bit of an asshole."

"John just cares a lot about his dog."

"Sure, but he brings his dog in here every week, and nothing's ever wrong with him."

"And yet today John and his dog left happy and content, and that's mostly because of Conall."

"I hear you," Liza said, with a nod. "You're right. To have someone like that running interference in the front office is huge." She shrugged. "If you want him, I can work with him," she muttered, "but it'll be awkward when I see him next."

"No, it won't be awkward at all. The only one who'll feel awkward is you, and that's because you didn't tell him anything," Bethany explained. "Yet now that we've told him, it's a done deal."

After saying goodbye to Liza, Bethany locked the door. Just as she went to head into the back to her office to deal with the paperwork that still needed to be done, Mel's mother, Kassie, drove up with the extra keys.

She hopped out, raced over, and gave them to her. "I'm so sorry to be this late. I've been trying to get here since we talked, but things were really crazy."

"Have you heard from Mel?"

She shook her head, tears in her eyes. "No, I haven't heard a thing from her, but I'm hearing all kinds of strange rumors now."

"Oh, you mean the fact her blasted boyfriend stole everything out of Michael's bank account, so they had something to run with?"

Her mother's jaw dropped. "Oh, please not, please, please, please not," she whispered. "Is that really true? … Her father will kill her."

"Yeah, well, it'll be a whole lot worse than that, since the law has been brought in on it now."

Kassie frowned. "Before she took off, she told me something about Page having every right to take the money from the account."

"*Really?*" Bethany asked, with a frown. "Page had been given access to Michael's bank account, so he could pay the bills because it's difficult for Michael to get out to make his own payments, given he's in a wheelchair and his vehicle has not yet been modified to accommodate that. Page also stole the money designated for Michael's property taxes."

"Oh, no. Even in a wheelchair he can barely maneuver," Kassie shared, tearing up again.

"Exactly, and, instead of helping Michael, Page went to the bank and took out all his money. Stole his car too."

She shook her head. "But that's so wrong, so wrong."

"Are you telling me that she knows better?" Bethany asked.

"I can tell you that she was raised better," Kassie whispered, "though I've got absolutely no excuses because I don't know how all that happened, and I don't know how to fix it. I have no idea what's got into her. Her father is raging like you wouldn't believe," Kassie shared, "so I need to go." And she turned and raced back to her vehicle.

Bethany looked down at her spare keys that had come from Mel's home, wondering if she should give them to Conall, then realizing she could just be making the same mistake all over again. As she looked at the keys, she noted something was off about them, and then it struck her. Some substance was stuck on them, and her heart sank. Knowing what it was, she immediately picked up her phone, took a photo of it, and sent it off to Conall.

He called her a few minutes later. "What is that?"

"I'm not sure. I was hoping you could confirm it for me. Mel's mother brought the keys, and I was grateful to have them, until I looked closer and saw what looks like a waxy substance on them."

"Like they took an impression of them?"

"I don't know for sure," she replied, "but I'm afraid so."

"Damn. Time to get the locks changed."

"I can't get anybody tonight," she cried out. "What are the chances that Mel and Page are still in town or are at least nearby?"

"Slim, but it doesn't matter," Conall stated. "I'll stay there tonight."

"What about Michael?"

He immediately started swearing.

"I know. That's how I feel too," she snapped in a fit. "I'll stay here."

"What? No, that's a bad idea."

"It's nothing. I mean, it's not like I have anything here for them to steal."

"You may not have any more *cash* for them to steal, but you do have equipment that they can sell and …" He hesitated, then said, "I presume you've got drugs."

"Oh my God," she cried out, "I wasn't even thinking of the medications, but, yes, I have a lot of those here."

"It could very well be next on their list."

"But that would just finish his reputation, if the cops ever catch him," she muttered. "If they do that, they'll be headed to the big-time crimes and the longer prison sentences that go with it."

"Exactly," Conall replied. "I don't want to leave Michael home alone either."

"That's what I mean, so I'll just stay here myself," she declared.

"Nope, that's too dangerous. See if we can get the locks changed tonight. If we can't, how do you feel about staying at Michael's place?"

She stared at her phone. "What? Why?"

"Because … the locks have been changed there already, so it's safer, and I'll stay at the vet clinic," he suggested in a wry tone. "That way we can keep all bases covered."

"You think there's a bigger chance of Page coming back here to the clinic than going to Michael's house?"

"Did you see the furniture at Michael's? I'm not sure there's a whole lot that Page can steal from there to sell, but at your clinic? It's a whole different story."

"God damn it," she muttered.

"Start making phone calls to see if you can get a locksmith, even if you have to pay an extra emergency fee to get it done tonight," he said. "This is not something we should fool around with."

"I'm on it, though I'm not sure how well it will go," she muttered. She disconnected and started pacing, as she phoned the one and only locksmith in town. He was not impressed. "I know, and I hear you, but it's not as if I accidentally lost my keys or something like that," she explained. "This is somebody I fired for stealing, and, while she still had the keys in her possession, it appears that she and her boyfriend have made an impression of these keys, at least that's what I assume from the sticky stuff I'm seeing on the keys themselves."

Silence came from the other end. "Now that's a whole different story," he muttered. "I guess I'm coming out to your place."

"Yes, please do."

"Are you there now?"

"I am," she confirmed.

"Okay, fine. I'll be there in about twenty minutes. Hang tight." And, with that, he hung up.

Sighing with relief, she immediately texted Conall back. **Crisis averted. Locksmith on his way now.**

She got a thumbs-up for her efforts, but it was enough. Just knowing that she had somebody else to even talk to about this whole mess gave her a false sense of security that this would all work out, when, of course, absolutely no way to know that anything would work out at all. This was a bad deal right from the start.

She should have listened to her gut and not hired Melanie to begin with. Now here she was, running up an expense she didn't need, on top of a minor theft that she also didn't need. Yet it really wasn't about the money; it was all about the betrayal. Apparently Mel had absolutely zero sense of right or wrong when it came to shit like that.

As soon as Bethany got off the phone, she headed back to her office to wait for the locksmith and to hope that maybe they could get this changed quickly.

As she sat down, she got busy on her paperwork, then heard an odd sound. She froze, but then realized it would be the locksmith and bolted out to the front. Instead of the locksmith, Mel walked in the door. Bethany glared at her. "What the hell are you doing here?"

Mel froze. "You're supposed to be gone," she cried out.

"Guess what," Bethany snapped, her temper flaring, "I'm not." Right behind Melanie was Page. "And you," she added, holding back her anger, "you asshole. How dare you steal from your uncle, leaving him with nothing, and now here you are breaking into my place. What the hell?"

"We didn't break in," he replied, with a smug smile. "She's got keys."

"She's also been fired and using them now is burglary, even if you didn't break in," she clarified. "You're still stealing."

"I haven't touched nothing," he pointed out, looking at her with a cocky smile, "so I don't know what you're talking about."

She looked back at Mel. "What are you doing, Mel? What are you making of your life? Your mom has been trying to get a hold of you all day."

Mel snorted. "The only reason is so she can yell at me. Why the hell would I even pick up the phone for that?"

"Do you think this is a game?" Bethany asked her. "People are getting hurt. Like Michael, when you stole his money."

Mel argued, "No I didn't." She looked over at Page now.

"I didn't either," the gangly kid argued cheerfully. "He gave me access."

"So, you think that because he gave you access to pay his bills, it was okay to take his money for yourself?"

He shrugged. "It doesn't matter. Besides, that's small potatoes compared to the stuff you've got here."

"And you think I'll just sit here and let you take it?" she asked in astonishment. But what he did next was something she never dreamed would ever happen.

He pulled out a gun and immediately fired one shot at her feet.

He grinned at her shocked look, as she hopped back. "Yeah, I think you are."

CONALL WALKED ALONG the road, trying to figure out where the War Dog would have gone. It was a fairly inhospitable landscape off to the side from the parking lot. Working backward, Bacchus would have taken off outside, but that didn't mean he would have gone anywhere in particular. He knew this place and this town, so chances were, wherever he had gone was exactly wherever he wanted to be, and that was what Conall didn't know. As he kept wandering along, he watched the vehicles, but the road was calm and fairly quiet. There was traffic, but it wasn't hard or intense.

When he got to a gas station up ahead, he walked in and asked if they had seen Bacchus. He had a picture of him, which he showed the attendant.

The man looked at it and nodded. "Yeah, I've seen him. It was a few days back now. I've seen him a couple times now. He comes in with Danny."

"Danny," Conall repeated. "Who's Danny?"

He shrugged. "Danny is one of the neighbors up here." He pointed down the road. He hesitated. "He wouldn't have done anything to hurt the dog."

"Maybe not, but the dog was easily spooked, and the owner is a war veteran, entrusted to look after the dog. So now that Bacchus has gone missing, it's caused a lot of upset everywhere."

"You're likely to have a lot of upset with Danny too." The attendant winced. "I might as well just tell you. Danny's got Down syndrome. He's in his forties, and, ever since he found the dog, he's been all over it."

Conall studied him and nodded. "That would explain why nobody has seen him."

"Oh, a lot of people have seen him, but they haven't mentioned anything about it." The man smiled. "Danny is harmless, and, if anything makes him happy, most people are inclined to let him have it."

"Sure, but this is not his dog."

"I'm not so sure about that because I've seen him with that dog a lot over the last few months. Maybe we're talking about a completely different dog," he suggested, glancing back at the photo. He shrugged. "I can't be sure it's the same dog."

"I have to check it out, so where will I find Danny?" When the man hesitated, Conall added, "I'm not trying to cause trouble, but we have a retired military veteran who needs the dog for support to help Michael get through the day. I understand that Danny may have fallen in love with Bacchus too, but we also need to ensure that Bacchus is well looked after."

"I'm pretty sure that Danny's got him, and he's looked after and much more."

"Maybe, and maybe there is a way they can share the dog," Conall suggested. "The War Department sent me to find the War Dog, and, if it wasn't me, it would be somebody else."

"Right, so you're not going away?"

"No, I'm not going away," he confirmed, with a small smile. He turned to look directly at the man. "So, where will I find Danny?"

He sighed, then shrugged. "He just lives up the road here." He pointed out the back. "I don't have an address for him, but I know he's somewhere around there. You can always see him outside walking, especially now that he's got the dog."

"Right," Conall noted. "It could be a lot worse news. I mean, Bacchus could have been run over by a car again. I understand he had an incident with a car not long ago."

"Right," he agreed, now brightening, "but I sure as hell don't know anything about that. Yet I do know that Danny looks after the dog really well."

"I'm glad to hear that," Conall said. "I'll go easy. I promise."

"You do that because Danny really is harmless."

"Good to know. Does he have a mom here or family?"

"He does, and she works at the corner store down there, which is why you often see Danny hanging around there too."

"Okay, good enough." Conall turned to walk out but then added, "Don't call him to let him know I'm coming, please. No need to delay the inevitable."

The man flushed, his hand immediately pulling back from the phone, like he'd been in the process of grabbing it.

Conall nodded. "It'll just prolong the process, if I have to hunt him down again, if you do call, and if they decide to hide him. If they know that I'm coming about the dog, it'll upset everybody, and we don't need that."

"No, no," he muttered thoughtfully. "I guess not. It's your business, you and Danny, I guess."

"If it isn't his dog, he doesn't get to keep it, and you might want to think about Michael, who owns the dog."

"If he lost him …"

Conall cut him off. "Michael's an older disabled veteran in a wheelchair, and his nephew had taken Bacchus to be checked out at the animal clinic, after the earlier incident with the car, but he lost him."

"Right. … That would make a stupid kind of sense, wouldn't it?"

"Not to me, and maybe not to you, but to the nephew? Well, … he's kind of a loser, if you ask me."

The man snorted. "Yeah, kin can often be trouble," he shared. "Go find Danny and talk to him, but I am telling you that he's a good person."

"I'm glad to hear it." Conall smiled and left.

As he headed back outside, he walked in the direction of the corner store. As he approached, vehicles were coming and going from there continuously. The store must be doing a good business, as it was bustling. He walked inside, noting the woman at the cash register. He smiled at her, as he walked up. "Hey, are you Danny's mom?"

She nodded, returning a smile. "Yep, I sure am. What's he done now?"

Conall chuckled. "I don't know," he replied, "but I understand he picked up a new dog a while back."

"The dog was lost," she explained, a frown on her face. "Danny's just been looking after him."

"That's good," Conall noted, "because that's a lost War Dog."

She stilled and looked at him. "He really loves that dog."

She seemed to know where this conversation was headed.

"I understand that," he said, cutting her off, "but somebody else loves the dog too. I don't suppose you know an older veteran named Michael."

Her face beamed. "Yeah, I do. I used to know him quite well, way back when, but then … he came home from the war, and life got in between us. My husband got sick, and life wasn't so easy, so I kind of lost track of Michael."

Conall nodded. "I understand. Michael is having a pretty rough time of it right now, and that nephew, who was supposed to be here helping him, well, he's no good."

"Yeah, I could have told Michael that," she snapped. "When I saw that punk around town and realized who it was, I had two minds on whether I should call Michael and ask him what the hell he was doing with that loser here but decided against it."

"Maybe you should call him now because he's feeling pretty beat up and abused by the world."

She immediately came around the counter, her arms wrapped around her chest, as she asked, "What happened?"

When he explained it to her, she gasped in horror. "Oh my God, Danny would never have taken the dog, if he'd known that was going on."

"And yet"—Conall looked directly at her—"I believe that dog has been regularly going to your place for a long time now, like weeks and even months."

She flushed. "But we didn't know it was Michael's. The dog would come up to the door, and Danny would open it. He eventually started coming in. After that, he would come and visit for a while. Then he would go to the door, and he would leave again."

"It all started happening more when the nephew showed

up in town," Conall explained.

"Well, damn, that young man has a lot to answer for."

"He does, but that doesn't mean that he'll answer for any of it because you know what the law is like around here. I've only been here a few days, and I've seen plenty that should have been dealt with but hasn't been."

"Michael needs to ensure his nephew pays for it."

"Agreed, but Michael's feeling pretty vulnerable at the moment. Somebody he chose to trust just stole every penny he had, and his beloved pet is gone, and now he's all alone. That's not exactly the kind of thing we want him to be feeling right now. Not on top of the heavy load he already carries."

Her shoulders sagged, and she asked, "You want me to take the dog from Danny and bring him home, right?"

"What do you think? You know Michael."

"I've known Michael a long time," she admitted. "I didn't know it was his dog though."

"You didn't really care to find out either, did you?" he pointed out.

She flushed and added, "It's hard enough just looking after Danny."

"Understood," Conall noted, "and I'm not trying to upset Danny either, but I do need to know that Michael will be okay."

She ran her hand through her hair. "I should have messaged him a long time ago about that nephew of his."

"How did you know he was trouble?"

"I caught him stealing here at the store," she shared. "I caught him stealing and told him to get his ass out of here, or I would press charges. I haven't seen him since."

"It's too bad you didn't press charges because now he's

cleaned out Michael's bank account. Page and his girlfriend stole from the animal clinic too."

"Shit," she muttered. "I'll go talk to Michael."

"Why don't you get Danny too and bring Bacchus over to Michael's place? But you and Danny both need to understand that Bacchus needs to be where he was placed. I was sent here to find him and to get him home."

She hesitated and then nodded slowly. "I may as well tell you. Michael and I had a thing going on years ago. … I didn't realize it was so bad for him now."

"I think he's hit rock bottom, and he's trying to figure out how to find his way back up again. However, he's got to care in order to be motivated to make that climb."

She stared at him, her jaw working slowly. "I'm definitely calling him then," she snapped. "He went off to war, and I married somebody else instead." She shook her head. "I just couldn't be a war bride, never knowing if he would come home again."

"He came home in pretty rough shape and has been going downhill. I know he would really appreciate it if somebody would reach out a hand and would show him some kindness, you know?"

"Done." She immediately picked up the phone and dialed a number, which went to voice mail. "Danny, answer the damn phone, will you?"

When his voice came through the phone, she smiled and asked, "Hey, have you've got the dog with you?"

Conall heard Danny's voice in the background, happily chatting away. "Bring him to the store, honey." She looked back at Conall and asked him, "Where's your vehicle?"

"I'm parked nearby the vet clinic, where he went missing from."

She nodded. "It'll take Danny a little bit to get here, so go get your vehicle and come on back."

He hesitated and she shrugged. "Look. I don't have any ax to grind, and, if I'd realized it was Michael's dog, I would have brought him home. I would have stopped him from coming over, but it seemed like the dog wasn't liking life very much."

"Again, we're back to the nephew …" Conall said.

"Yeah," she muttered, "he was trouble right from the start."

"Agreed, and now he's just in bigger trouble." Conall looked at his watch and added, "I'll be back in about twenty minutes."

"Good enough," she said. "I'll keep Danny in the dark here. I don't know how it will go, but he'll be pretty upset."

"Maybe he can come to Michael's house with me, and we can be part of the same reunion."

She raised her eyebrows. "That could work, and I'm off here in about half an hour anyway."

"So, maybe you should come over and see him too."

She smiled. "It's been a long time."

"Yeah, it's been a long time for Michael too. It's hard to come home from the war broken, disabled, and knowing that everybody hates you because you're a reminder of what they should have done but didn't."

"He was always stubborn, strong-headed, and willful," she shared, with a smile, "but he always had heart."

"And that hasn't changed."

"How bad is he?"

"He's in a wheelchair, missing one leg. I don't even know the extent of his injuries, but he should have been getting some care and some help, … and he hasn't been getting that either. I'm trying to see what his needs are and give him a hand."

"I appreciate that," she replied, "and thanks for the heads-up. We tend to bury our heads in the sand, and we don't do what we should."

"Yeah, you got that right."

With that, he lifted a hand and headed back out, feeling relieved that at least he had a line on the War Dog. He still had to see the dog to confirm that it was Bacchus and that he was healthy and well cared for. This was a better outcome than he could have hoped for. The fact that two people loved the dog could cause troubles, but maybe they could work something out together. He didn't know yet.

He walked back to his truck, got in, and headed to the vet clinic. Just as he came around the corner, he thought he saw a vehicle outside. As he got closer, he saw three people inside the big glass front doors. That had to be the locksmith. Deciding to confirm that the locks were changed to something more secure, he stepped up closer, heading down the parking lot. He froze when he realized who was there and that he was brandishing a gun. Instead of rushing forward, Conall stepped back and called the sheriff's office.

When he put his phone away, he crept around to the back door and tested it. Finding it locked, Conall pulled out his wallet, where he kept a tiny pick, and had the back door opened in seconds. Swearing at the terrible system she had, he walked through, calling out, "Hey, honey. I thought you would be home by now."

Dead silence came from the other room.

Conall walked straight through to the lobby, where the three of them stood. He nodded at Melanie. "Look at that," he stated. "We wondered if you'd taken a copy of the keys.

That's a felony by the way, so don't complain that you weren't warned."

"No, it's not," she argued, staring at him. "Where the hell did you come from?"

"Doesn't matter where I came from," he replied, eyeing her with interest. When he turned to Bethany, she was pale but had hope in her gaze, when she saw him. "And here I thought it was the locksmith working away in here."

"He's on his way," Bethany shared, with a nervous glance at Page.

At that, the nephew and Mel looked at each other and started to back out. "We'll be back," Page announced, with a laugh. "It's not like a lock will change anything." And, with that, he raced outside, dragging Mel with him. They got into the vehicle, laughing and giggling, as they tore off down the road.

Then Conall noted a bullet hole in the floor. He frowned, asking her, "Seriously?"

She nodded. "First thing he did was fire at my feet," she whispered. She looked at him, her gaze huge.

He opened his arms, and she collapsed into them, bawling.

# CHAPTER 9

BETHANY CALMED DOWN relatively quickly, mostly because the locksmith pulled in right after the two thieves had left. Wiping away her tears, she opened the door, and he hurried in.

"Hope it's really important. My after-hours rate isn't cheap."

"The people who just left are the ones who copied my keys, and they came in with a gun," she stated, still rubbing tears from her eyes.

He looked at her and whistled. "That's not good." Right behind him came the sheriff's deputy in a cruiser.

Bethany raised her eyebrows at Conall, and he nodded. "Yep, that was me." He smiled and went out to talk to them, while Bethany spoke to the locksmith.

The locksmith nodded. "Yeah, okay then. It's important. I'll get on it." He pointed to the entrance. "Just the front doors?"

She nodded, but then Conall returned, and she told him, "The locksmith just asked me if we should do only the front door."

Conall immediately shook his head. "No, you need to do the back door too."

"Why is that? I don't think she had a key to that door."

"I just picked that lock to come in, when I saw they had

a gun, and that only took about two seconds."

The locksmith faced him and swore. "He's right," he agreed, turning to Bethany. "You shouldn't have a lock that's so easy to pick."

"No, she shouldn't have, but I'm sure it wasn't on purpose," Conall added.

"Right," the locksmith muttered and got to work.

She walked over to Conall, and he wrapped an arm around her and held her close. "It's okay. We'll get this sorted out."

"It's not every day I face an armed intruder in my clinic or realize that I had accidently employed a psychopath in training."

"These hoodlums have just taken a big step," Conall noted, "and it's not a step that anybody is happy about."

"What did the deputy say?"

"They're out looking for them now. I gave them a brief description and license plate of the vehicle, but chances are they'll ditch it fairly quickly. At least you're getting your locks changed, so that's progress."

She nodded. "Somehow it doesn't feel like it's enough though, especially since Page warned me that they would be back. How the hell did you get in?" she whispered.

"As I said, I picked the lock on the back door," he repeated, staring at her. "Your system really does suck."

She raised her hands in frustration. "Thanks for that," she wailed, almost in tears again.

"You're welcome," he teased, nudging her, trying to get a smile, "but at least now we can get it fixed."

She shook her head and rubbed her face with her hands. "I just can't believe this day." She groaned. "I just want to go home, have a bath, and get to bed."

"You'll do that soon enough," he replied, "I, … on the other hand, found Bacchus, and I'll go introduce the person who has the dog to Michael."

She looked up at him in shock. "What? You found Bacchus?"

"I did," he confirmed. "Now I just have to find a way to make it all work out," he added. Then he explained what had happened.

"Oh my gosh, Danny is a sweetheart," she said. "Of course he's the one who would have found Bacchus."

"Or the other way around. Looks like maybe he's the one the War Dog has been visiting on a regular basis."

She nodded. "That would make sense, but it'll break Danny's heart, if he has to give up Bacchus."

"But the dog wasn't his in the first place."

"I know. I know," she conceded, holding up her hand. "You don't have to convince me of that. I just know it'll be hard on Danny."

"Maybe, or maybe he'll be totally okay with it. I don't know, but I also need to get back to Michael's place too."

"Of course," she agreed. "I'm here for now, and I'm fine."

He hesitated and then nodded. "I think you probably are for the moment. Get the locks changed, and let me know when you leave, so that I know where you are."

She smiled up at him. "You arrived in town just in time to help out, didn't you?"

"Or maybe I put it all into motion. Anyway," he added, with a shrug, "not that I intentionally tried to upend everything, but some things happen for a reason."

"I certainly believe that," she murmured, "and if I can do anything to help out, let me know."

"I'm still trying to keep an eye on Michael," Conall shared, "so if you come up with any solutions there, I'm all ears."

"Will do," she replied. She watched as he pulled away.

When the locksmith looked at her, she smiled. "He's been a godsend since he arrived."

"I can't believe he came after a War Dog, if that's what I was hearing."

"Yeah, he sure did. It's nice to know that somebody cares about them."

"Yeah, I wouldn't have thought so. The things they did to War Dogs back in Vietnam made me so angry. So I'm glad to see the government is treating them better now. I enlisted back then, but I walked away from that crap."

She winced. "That's a bit of history I don't want to know about."

"Sure, but it's also the history that we can't allow ourselves to forget," he stated, "any more than we can let back in again whoever you had in here tonight. With the medications you've gotta have here, you really should have a much better system."

"Apparently so," she muttered. "I just hadn't realized it was such a terrible system."

He smiled. "Now you know better. Let me go get the back door done, and then you should consider a full-on security system."

"I do have one," she shared, "and that's how I tend to keep track of everything here, but the doors weren't a part of it."

He grimaced and shook his head. "Then it's not a full-on system. It's half a system, and you need to get a whole lot more because, chances are, those kids will come back."

She bit her lip at that. "You really think so?"

"Yeah, I really do," he confirmed. "That's just the kind of people they are. You need to ensure that you're a whole lot safer when they do return and that you have a backup system to keep them out."

"Yet if they really wanted in," she noted, looking at him wryly, "they'll just shoot the locks out or break the windows, right?"

"Hopefully that would trigger an alarm and bring someone in to help you out," he replied. "Because you've got drugs here, that's a whole different ball game."

Feeling thoroughly chastised by everybody in her world by that point in time, she was happy when he was finally done. She paid the bill, wincing at the completely unexpected amount, yet knowing he was right.

"Now, get the security system people back in here and ensure that they connect the doors and windows and that there's an alarm in place, in case of a break-in."

She nodded, not knowing what else to say. A security company had set this up in the first place, but she had gone cheap because she hadn't had a whole lot of money. Thankfully that time had come and gone, and her practice was thriving, so she needed to do something a whole lot more serious about security.

Making a note to herself, she locked up and headed home. She was exhausted after a long day, and the last thing she needed now was to have her sleep interrupted because she had to come right back and start again tomorrow. She also hadn't checked to see if her volunteer helper would be around tomorrow or if he was done here. Considering he'd already found Bacchus, maybe Conall's stay was over, and that was another unsettling thought she didn't even want to consider.

Something was very capable, even magnetic about him, and the last thing Bethany wanted was to say goodbye to him now. She wasn't sure she had any choice though, and, if he had found Bacchus, there was a really good chance that Conall would be gone tomorrow, and that would break her heart.

CONALL DROVE BACK to the corner store, only to find the woman looking at him in exasperation. "You said you would come back in like fifteen or twenty minutes."

He quickly explained what had held him up, and she gasped. "What the hell were they thinking? Page had a gun and fired at Bethany? That's crazy."

"I know. Pretty ridiculous," he agreed, looking around. "How much longer is your shift?"

"I'm done now." She winced. "That's the last thing we need around here."

"Yeah, I'm pretty sure it's the last thing Bethany needed too."

"I hear you. Anyway, Danny is here, and he's got the dog."

"I need to see the dog to confirm it is Bacchus."

"He's out back. Danny sits out there and has an ice cream most of the time."

Conall nodded and headed out back, and, sure enough, the dog looked remarkably like the one in the pictures. He smiled.

As he walked out, the dog raced over on three legs to say hello, showing absolutely no fear or sign of distress. Danny came over as well, with a big smile on his face. "Hi," he said happily.

"Hi there, Danny. I was just talking to your mom."

He just nodded and didn't say anything, the big smile still on his face.

Conall felt terrible, knowing he had to let Danny know that the dog had to go back to Michael. Conall just shook his head because, at the moment, he couldn't see a path to making this work out because he wasn't prepared to let Michael suffer either. "How long have you had the dog?" he asked Danny.

"I found him," Danny replied. "He needed saving."

"Sure he did, and you did a great job. Did you try to find who he belonged to?"

He nodded. "We did, but nobody came forward."

He wondered how hard they'd really tried and guessed it wasn't much of an effort, but it wasn't for Conall to say. "Do you know Michael, the older man in town who lives in a wheelchair?"

Danny looked a little confused for a moment and then shrugged. "I don't think so."

"He had a dog like this."

Danny stared at him. "Like this one?"

He nodded. "Yeah, just like this one."

Danny frowned and shook his head. "I don't think *like this one*. This one is special."

"He is, isn't he?" Conall agreed, with a bright smile. He looked around to see Danny's mom standing there, biting her lip. Conall took several photos of the dog and then called him by name.

Bacchus immediately turned on a dime, his ears up, and he gave a *woof.* Conall smiled and called him over. Bacchus raced over and welcomed him with a huge welcome, even more than he had done before, as if understanding that somebody knew who he was.

He gave the dog a big cuddle, laughing as Bacchus tumbled Conall to the ground in his joy. As he looked up, Danny frowned at him, asking, "Does he know you?"

"He certainly knows *of* me," he said, with a gentle smile. He looked over at his mother and nodded.

She sighed. "Danny, let's go get into the car, and we're taking Bacchus with us."

"Okay. Where are we going?"

"We'll go see Michael."

Danny shrugged. "Why?"

"Because we've got to see if Bacchus is his."

At that, Danny shook his head. "No, no, he's mine."

"We know he's not yours," his mom explained, brooking no arguments, "and just imagining that he's yours doesn't make it so."

Danny looked terrified for a moment, and his mother reminded him, "We always knew that he could belong to somebody else because he was looked after and healthy. It's not right to keep him, honey."

"But, if he wanted to go back, he would have, like he did before."

"That's because somebody was at home that he didn't like, but that person is gone now. So we'll go and take him to his owner."

"Do you think he would let me keep him?" he asked hopefully.

His mom hesitated, then shrugged. "I wouldn't count on it, honey. He needs the dog too."

At that, Danny immediately got belligerent. "No, no,

no, the dog is mine."

His mom refused to argue with him. "Get in the car, Danny," she repeated. "We're heading over there now, and, if this dog is his, we'll have a talk with him."

"Only if talking to him means I get to keep him," Danny stated, glaring at her.

It took some work, but they finally got Danny and Bacchus into her car.

"You can follow me," Conall suggested.

"I know where Michael lives," she shared in a casual tone. "I've driven past a couple times over the years. I should have just stopped in, damn it."

"Now you get a chance," Conall pointed out.

She nodded, and he raced to his truck. The fact that Bacchus was as happy as he was revealed a lot about his relationship with Danny, but it didn't change the fact that Michael was desperately in need of this dog. By the time Conall made it to Michael's place, he pulled into the driveway and saw Michael open his front door, relief evident on his face.

"You okay, Michael?" Conall asked.

"I am, but my nephew was here."

Conall groaned. "Did he hurt you?"

"No, he didn't hurt me, but I don't know what's wrong with that kid. He came through, grabbed his stuff, and left, telling me that I couldn't stop him and that I didn't have any right to the money and that I gave it to him. Conall, can you do something, please? I didn't give it to him. I told him that I needed it for food and the property taxes and that he knew I didn't have much money. But, to him, when he looked at the account, I had lots of money, so, like everybody else, I was lying."

"Yet what he thinks is *a lot* won't be a lot at all in the real world, will it?"

"No, but he doesn't have any concept of how much it really takes to live," Michael said. "So, from his perspective, maybe it was a lot." Michael just shook his head. "I don't know. It's just all bad."

"It is bad. I'll agree with you on that." Just then another vehicle drove in behind him.

Michael looked out and asked, "Who's this?"

"Somebody from your past," Conall replied, with a smile, and he watched as Danny's mom got out.

She looked over at him and smiled heartily. "Hey, Michael."

He looked at her in surprise. "Mariam?"

She nodded. "Yeah, it's me." She walked up closer to him and then stopped and called out, "Come on, Danny. Hop out."

Danny just shook his head.

"I'll go get him," Conall offered. He walked to her car and opened up the passenger door. "You don't have to come out, Danny, but Bacchus does." And, with that, Conall called Bacchus, who immediately hopped out and raced to the front door, barking the whole time, as he happily greeted Michael.

Michael, with tears in his eyes, immediately wrapped his arms around the dog, hugging him, and he couldn't stop crying. He frowned at Mariam. "Did you have my dog?"

"We didn't know it was your dog," she explained. "Danny found him out on the highway."

Confused and obviously not sure what this turn of events meant, Michael looked at Danny, who was still in the car. Danny finally got out and walked over. Then Michael understood. "Ah, you're looking good," he said to Mariam, as he gazed back at her.

She smiled. "I'm a little worse for wear. It's not as if life has been easy on me," she muttered.

He nodded. "Danny is yours?"

She nodded. "Yeah, he's all I've got."

"Life hasn't been easy on either of us, has it?"

"No, it really hasn't."

He invited them all in, as he looked over at Conall. "I'm amazed, man. You really found him, didn't you?"

"I did," he confirmed. "As you can see, it's a bit of a situation."

"I can see that." Michael nodded. "I'm not sure what I'm supposed to do about it."

"Right now, you don't have to do anything. Bacchus is yours."

"Right," Michael agreed, "but it seems somebody else is affected by a loss here too."

"I know." Conall nodded.

"I'm not even sure what to do with this turn of events," Michael admitted, "and I'll need a bit of help to try and figure it out."

"We'll figure it out," Conall vowed, placing a hand on the older man's shoulder.

With everybody inside the house, Conall bent over and spent some time getting to know Bacchus. It was pretty easy, since Bacchus was a happy-go-lucky, well-settled dog, which spoke volumes about his care in both homes.

He smiled when he looked at the way Michael got along with the dog and with the way Bacchus interacted with Michael. Conall turned to look at Michael. "I gather your nephew caused all the trouble with Bacchus?"

Michael nodded. "I didn't realize what was happening. Page kept telling me that the dog was disappearing, but now I don't know whether he was really taking off on his own or if Page was trying to get rid of him."

"Most likely Page was trying to get rid of Bacchus because that isolated you, making it easier for you to become more dependent on Page."

Mariam gasped, looking at Michael. "I considered contacting you a couple times, but I didn't know how to tell you this. Your nephew came in and stole from the store. I caught him at it and told him to never come back," she shared. "I should have mentioned something to you, but a lot of years have gone by, and it was a little awkward to reach out and say *Hi* in that circumstance."

"I wish you had," he stated. "Page came in and cleaned me out. The truth is, I wouldn't even have dinner tonight if it wasn't for this man here," he admitted sadly. "When you get old, and you're broken, people just want to take advantage of you. I keep thinking I've seen the worst of humanity, then my own family shows me a new low."

Mariam nodded and smiled sadly. "I've very sorry I didn't, but I'm very glad that, in the end, this situation did bring me here, and I'm very happy to see you."

He looked at her and grinned. "You didn't used to be so shy," he teased. "In the old days, you would have come right over to say *Hello*."

"Yeah," she agreed, "but that was before I had Danny."

Understanding crossed his face, and he nodded. "I would have done the same thing," he conceded, "but that was also before I came home from the war like this."

They smiled at each other, and even Conall could see a romance blossoming. "I'm really glad you two have reconnected. I'm hoping the two of you can work out a way to maybe allow Danny some playdates with Bacchus here."

Mariam looked at him and then back at Michael. "Or Danny and I could just come over and visit."

"That would be even better," Michael agreed. "Honest to God, life has been pretty damn lonely, and I would be happy to have you come over anytime. I knew you were working down at the grocery store, but, like you, I didn't go to see you."

"I understand," she replied, "but we're past that part, and we can keep in touch now."

"I would say so," Michael said, "plus you were always one hell of a cook."

She flushed at that. "Yeah, but I don't have anybody to cook for anymore," she said, with a sigh. "I mean, I have Danny, but honestly he prefers chicken fingers."

Danny smiled. "I love chicken fingers."

She nodded. "I know you do, honey."

Danny looked over at Michael. "You know my mom?"

Michael nodded. "Yes. We were friends a long time ago."

Mariam put a hand on Michael's shoulder. "We're still friends. It just seems as though we had a few things to get past."

"And are we past them now?" Michael asked. "I have a hard time believing you don't have people knocking down your door." He eyed her, a twinkle in his gaze. "Because it would sure be nice to know somebody out there gave a damn."

"Somebody out there does give a damn," she confirmed, smiling. "I just didn't expect to have this happen. It's been lonely for me too. Most people I've met haven't wanted to deal with Danny."

"No reason not to," Michael replied. "He looks like a good young man."

"He is, but he can also be a challenge."

"Yeah, … well, I've got my own challenges these days," Michael noted, as he patted the wheelchair he was sitting in. "Nothing easy about this either."

That brought up a discussion about what had happened to Michael and how he'd gotten injured, so he quickly told her about the IED the truck ran over and how long Michael had been dealing with this mess. She was more than shocked, and Conall felt like a fly on the wall, as the two rekindled their friendship from such a long time ago. Yet, at the end of the evening, he'd managed to turn a no-win situation into a massive win for all concerned, including Bacchus.

Not only was a friendship once again opening on both sides but Danny could also use somebody in his world, and, from the looks of it, Bacchus was more than happy to have both of them in his world.

Just then Conall's phone rang. *Bethany.* He answered it and asked, "Hey, did you get the locks changed?"

"Yes, I did get the locks changed on the clinic." Then her voice changed, becoming almost cautious. "But I'm sitting outside my place, and there's a light on, and I know I didn't leave one on."

He froze. "Where are you right now?"

"I'm in my vehicle," she muttered, "and honestly, Conall, … I'm too scared to go inside."

"Don't go inside," he snapped. "I'm on my way."

"Are you sure?" she asked, her voice nervous. "I should be calling the sheriff."

"I'll be there in five minutes," he stated. "Stay outside,

locked in your car. You hear me?"

"What should I do about the sheriff?"

"Call them but nobody else. And, if anybody comes, you keep your car windows closed, your car doors locked, keep your engine running—in case you have to pull out of there. If you do have to leave, you tell me right away. Do you hear me? I don't want to show up and find you not there."

"I promise." Then she added, "Please hurry. A second light just went on."

"I'm on my way." And, with that, Conall looked at Michael, then Mariam, Danny, and Bacchus. "Can you guys work this out?"

Michael looked at him, his gaze hard. "What's going on, Conall?"

"Your nephew recently got his hands on a gun, and he's starting to use it to his advantage."

All the color drained from Michael's face. "Go," he said. "Page is a stupid punk-ass kid, but he sure doesn't need to die, just as he learns to grow up."

"It might be too late for that," Conall shared. "Page has already pulled a gun on Bethany once and shot at her feet. Now we think he's at her apartment."

"Run," Michael ordered, "run."

And, with that, Conall didn't hesitate, bolting out the door. He slammed into his vehicle, hit Reverse, even while he was ordering his phone to dial Badger's number. By the time he was connected, Conall was already three-quarters of the way there. In terse tones, he gave Badger an update on what was happening.

"As soon as you get there," Badger said, "you let us know just how bad it is."

"I'm two seconds away," he added, speeding as fast as he

could. "I'll let you know." And, with that, he hung up, peeled into the apartment parking lot, and froze.

He saw no sign of Bethany or her car.

# CHAPTER 10

BETHANY DIDN'T WANT to stay parked where she was so obviously exposed, especially in case whoever was inside her place could see her. So Bethany put her vehicle into Reverse and backed out of the spot that she normally used and pulled around the corner. There she stopped and waited, hoping that Conall would show up sooner than later.

It made her angry to think that somebody was in her place, but, more than that, it terrified her. Was Page really that stupid? He was headed down a pathway that would get him into some big trouble, but, for everybody's sake, it would be nice if they could stop it before he went too far. Doing shit like this wouldn't help or make anybody's day. Even as she watched anxiously, her palms started to sweat, while waiting and waiting for Conall to show up. When she saw a vehicle that looked remarkably like his, she let out a breath of air, sagging back in her seat.

"Finally," she muttered, then realized that he didn't know where she was. She flashed her lights, hoping he would see that, and, within a few seconds, his lights flashed back.

She grinned. "Always nice to work with somebody who understands," she muttered. As he drove closer, she hopped out of her vehicle and ran toward him. He pulled up, shut off the engine to his truck, hopped out, and opened his arms.

She immediately bailed into them, feeling a sense of security that she hadn't felt in a very long time. When she looked up at him, tears were in her eyes. "Sorry, I didn't know who else to call," she muttered.

"It's fine," he said. "You did the right thing."

She rolled her eyes. "You know the sheriff won't agree with that."

"I've brought them in on a few things already, so they're probably ready for me to leave town."

She nodded. "Maybe, but it will be a sad day for the rest of us when you do."

He looked at her and then smiled. "It's nice to know I'll be missed."

"Oh, you'll be missed," she confirmed instantly. "You've made yourself right at home, from the moment you arrived."

"Not intentionally," he murmured, "this has never been what I thought I would be doing."

"So, tell me more about Bacchus."

HE GLANCED AROUND and realized that they were literally only a block or two from where Bacchus and Michael were. "I wonder how is it that you didn't see Bacchus from here. He would have been going past this place during the day."

"Exactly. It's the *during the day* part. Remember?" she asked. "I'm at work."

"Right, that makes sense."

He wondered if there was any way to get Bacchus here, but it was probably better not to involve the dog, since Conall didn't know how good Bacchus was at following commands, especially after being out of regular work and training all this time.

He would love to work with him though. At least enough to make sure that all three of the people—Mariam, Michael, and Danny—involved with Bacchus going forward knew how to work him, because nothing was worse than having a dog with exceptional skills and not put them to good use. Especially if it meant the dog could do something to help save them when they got into trouble.

He chuckled, then looked back at her place. "I will fill you in on Bacchus, but I think we need to deal with this first."

"What is it we're dealing with anyway?" she asked, as she stared at the lights still on in her apartment. "How do we even know who's in there?"

"I would suggest," Conall said, "that we go find out."

She grabbed his arm and held him back. "What if they've got a gun?" she asked, and then she hesitated. "We already know for a fact that Page has one and doesn't mind using it. I don't want to insult you, but you've got a prosthetic."

He frowned at his leg and shrugged. "So what?" he asked. "I got it fighting a war overseas. I would just as soon have fought a war closer to home and had the same results," he admitted. "Believe me when I say that war is exactly what we're talking about here. Whether we like it or not, something bizarre is going on here because I can't see that kid doing what he's doing without somebody else pushing him to do it." And, with that, he held out a hand. "Come on. Let's get up to your place."

"Do you think we should call the sheriff again?"

"I've already told Badger. He is my liaison with the War Department, so he's getting somebody over here."

"Oh, good," she muttered, shuddering. "The deputy

didn't seem all that concerned when I called."

"I presume they'll listen to Badger, even if they won't listen to us."

"The fact that you think they won't even listen to you is already horrific," she noted, frowning at him.

"Very few people cross Badger and get away with it," he shared, with a chuckle. "I don't know whether you've got crooked cops, lazy cops, or just really overworked cops. However, I'm willing to give them the benefit of the doubt, although we should have company already, and nobody's here."

"I know," she muttered. "I called them what seems like ages ago. I had hoped they would get here before you and deal with it, so you didn't have to."

"Oh, that's kind of you," he teased, with a knowing nod, "but unfortunately, in a case like this, that's often where we're at."

"It shouldn't be," she declared.

"No, it shouldn't be, but that doesn't change things, does it?"

She glanced up at her second-floor apartment. "But we don't know who's in there waiting for us."

"No, we don't, and they probably don't know that we know about them either. Although having left lights on makes it unusual for them to still be there."

She shook her head. "Still, it seems like a really bad idea."

"Maybe it is, and we don't have to go up, if you don't want to." He stepped away from Bethany. "I'll go in and check it out."

"No, no, no, no," she argued. "You're not doing that."

He smiled. "Unless they're prepared to kill us and to go

really hardcore into whatever nasty little slide they are on, they'll have to find some way to deal."

"But what if Page *is* prepared to kill us?"

"Then I want you to stay here," he said, "and honestly you shouldn't be here at all." He considered the building in front of them. "Why don't you go back to your vehicle and stay there?"

"No. No way I'm letting you go in there alone."

He glanced at her sideways. "You want to wait for the deputy?"

She nodded. "I want *us* to wait for the deputy."

"And if the cops don't come?"

She winced. "I'm really hoping that's not the case."

Suddenly the decision was taken from them, when a gun nudged Conall in the back. He stiffened and a voice came, hard, yet barely a whisper. "Don't bother turning around, you cripple."

He didn't say anything, but glanced down at Bethany. She was staring up at him, horror in her gaze. He gave her a reassuring smile. "Easy now," he said, recognizing Jake's voice.

"Yeah, *easy*," Jake said in a mocking tone, "like what the hell? Would you just get your asses into the building, please? We've all been waiting around long enough."

Conall nodded and led the way up front. Bethany followed, her hand gripping his tightly. With his free hand diving into his pocket, he grabbed his phone and managed to find the Redial button, while they were pushing their way into the building, making it look like they couldn't quite get all three of them through at the same time. Conall was shoved to one side and told to get the hell out of the way and again called a cripple.

He wondered what kind of people took advantage of those weaker than themselves. It certainly wasn't Conall's style, but it seemed like they had a bad batch of that type in this town.

She looked over at him, but he had managed to hit Redial and left his phone in his pocket. He knew that Badger would figure it out pretty fast. If there was one thing he could count on, it was Badger's response. "What is it you want from us?" Conall asked, trying for a nervous voice.

At the sound of his tone, she looked at him in horror, but he gave her a wink, so she settled somewhat.

"You're causing trouble, that's what. So it's time for you to learn a lesson."

"Really? And what kind of lesson do you think you'll teach us?"

"You'll see soon enough."

Conall rolled his eyes, turning to Bethany. "You don't have an elevator?" Conall asked her.

She shook her head, frowning at Conall. "No, we don't have an elevator. I've been planning on moving. The lack of an elevator is kind of a pain, but it's just … It's only the second floor, and I've been really busy."

Prodding them, Jake muttered, "Shit, stop bitching. You'd be in much better shape if you were on the fourth floor, you know."

She didn't say anything but glared straight ahead.

"Then again," Conall told the gunman, "just imagine what kind of shape you would be in if you weren't using a gun to make people do what you wanted. I mean, you could get a job and be a decent person."

"I don't need to be a decent person, and I don't need to listen to your shit," Jake snapped. "Work is for losers."

"Or for people who want money."

"I get all the money I need," Jake snapped again, "and it sure as hell doesn't come from working."

"That's interesting. What kind of tricks do you have that you can get money without working for it? I may need to learn that myself."

Jake snorted. "Just shut the fuck up," he roared.

AT THE SECOND floor, they opened the door at the top of the stairwell, and Conall was the first to go through. They walked forward until they came to her apartment door, where she stopped and looked at Jake. "You want me to open it?" she asked him.

"Yes, I want you to open it," Jake declared, staring at her in amazement, "Shit, I would never bring an animal to you."

"Ah, so you do know who I am," she muttered. "I wondered. I also know who you are, Jake. I wondered if my lovely assistant and her boyfriend had something to do with this."

"She's a piece of cake, isn't she?" Jake laughed. "We'll put her to good use for now, but then she's done. We don't need that kind of brainlessness around us. We need women who can think for themselves, not like Mel."

"Oh, and here I thought you just wanted women who *didn't* think for themselves," she replied, with a fake laugh. "You know, the kind you can beat up and brutalize and have them coming back for more."

"Yeah, … well, that gets pretty tiring after a while," Jake muttered. "It's fun to start, but it gets boring quickly."

She shook her head, feeling the anger surge up her

throat. "Too bad, but, if you were more of a man," she snapped, "you could get yourself a real woman."

"Oh, one like you, I suppose," he said, with a jeer. "Look at you, standing there, holding hands with a cripple. If you were all woman, you wouldn't need to be picking up a cripple like that. You could get a real man yourself, though you are kind of old."

She stared at him and then started to laugh. "Good God," she muttered, "do you believe all that drivel you keep spouting?"

Jake smacked her hard across the face.

She bolted backward, holding her hand over her cheek, only to see a second guy exit her apartment, knocking Conall to his knees.

CONALL BRACED HIMSELF, ready to get up, when Jake pressed his gun against Conall's temple.

"Don't even think about it," he said. "I ain't got no patience for you right now."

"Really?" Conall asked, looking up at him. "Looks to me like you've got loads of trouble already."

"No, I don't, and I'm not interested in your opinion," he declared. "This is a warning, and we'll be back, if you don't listen and stay the hell out of our business."

He snorted. "What business? What did we ever do to you?" He stared at him. "What are you doing? Other than hassling the locals and not paying for coffee?" he asked, with a smile. "Is that seriously the level of crimes you guys are involved in?"

"I would be careful, if I were you," Jake growled.

"Yeah, I'm shocked at the audacity. Here you are, waving a gun around, because you're scared of getting caught shoplifting?" Conall stared at him. "That's pretty low, but I guess that's all you guys do. It's like your specialty, right?"

If glaring could kill, Conall would be dead by now. "You ain't got the balls or the brains to do anything else."

Jake's gun hand came up again, with the pistol directed at Conall's face.

Conall shook his head. "I wouldn't do that again," he said. "You've been getting away with these nonsense crimes because you're young and stupid, but, after this, it ain't happening."

Jake swore. "You don't know anything about us."

"No, I sure don't, and I don't really want to either. I mean, anybody can see *stupid* coming at them," he stated, "so the fact that you guys can't is seriously amazing."

"What?" Jake stared at Conall, wild-eyed, clutching the gun harder and harder.

"No," his cohort yelled.

Conall trained his gaze on Jake's buddy, and Conall could see fear in his partner's expression.

"We leave him alone," his buddy told Jake. "It was a warning, just a warning."

"You guys still haven't told me what the warning is about though," Conall repeated, staring at Jake. "How am I supposed to know what to avoid, if you don't tell me?"

"Consider yourself warned, cripple. We won't say it again."

"Oh, I get it now. You're hooked up with that punk-ass kid Page, who is driving things into the ground here in town."

At that, they looked at each other and asked, "What are

you talking about?"

"You think you're the only gunmen in town raising hell? No, you've got competition now," he revealed, with a smile. "Stupid competition, but then you guys don't look like you're all that bright either."

"What the fuck are you talking about?" Jake muttered.

Conall glanced over at Bethany, who even now still held her cheek. His gaze hardened. "I won't fucking tell you, not after you hit her like that. You're nothing but a coward. Don't worry if you don't find him. … I'm guessing Page will find you soon enough."

And, with that, he pushed Jake back and stood, then walked over to put his arms around Bethany. When he turned to look back, he told Jake and his buddy, "Get lost. If you're here to give us a warning, you've given it, so get the hell out."

The two men stared at him, nonplussed, as if this reaction was the opposite of what they expected, but Conall didn't give a shit. He was more concerned about Bethany and the blow to her cheek. He glared at them. "That's *your* last warning, now get the fuck out of here."

Both men seemingly took his advice and disappeared. When the door slammed behind them, he wrapped her tighter in his arms.

# CHAPTER 11

"HOW'S YOUR FACE?" Conall asked Bethany.

She shook her head. "It's fine," she muttered, still in shock. "I just can't believe it. They are so young, and they didn't used to be like that."

"No, men like that? They grow into it," Conall noted. "They think that they're something special and that nobody can stop them, and that's a fostered misbelief that they've gotten from family and friends." Conall shook his head. "It just lives in their world."

"It's worrisome what they said about Melanie," Bethany shared.

"I know. It's hard to tell what is truth and what is BS, but they surely knew who you were talking about. But it wasn't that clear whether Jake and his merry band are really hooked up with Page and Mel or not. Their egos are so big they're seriously looking for trouble, and, if they want it, they will find it," Conall said. "I really don't care at this point. I'm tired of dealing with the whole bunch of them."

She gave him half a smile. "But they got in here on their own."

"Yeah, remember that thing about locks?" he reminded her.

She groaned. "I don't even want to think about changing these too."

"Yet you also don't want them coming back."

"Do you really think a lock will change that?"

"No, I sure don't," he agreed. "We have to fix what's wrong here, and unfortunately that won't be an overnight process. Unless of course," he added, with a smirk, "they all end up finding each other."

"I don't know whether that's a good idea or not," Bethany replied, looking worried. "Page is so insistent on being the big man. If he comes up against one of these other groups, there will likely be a shootout."

Conall raised one eyebrow and asked innocently, "Is that so bad?"

She winced. "Stop it. I get that, for you, it's probably a perfect ending. However, for those of us around here, … who remember the younger and happier versions of these bullies, it'll be a much harder ending."

"One they all deserve," he stated.

She groaned. "I know. I know, but all I'm seeing right now is you being pissed that I got hurt."

He nodded. "Good, I'm glad you can see that because I am beyond pissed that you got hurt. Jake had no business hitting you like that."

"No," she agreed, as she moved her jaw tenderly. "I sure as hell wish he had missed that step."

"Trust me. He'll wish he had," Conall vowed.

She looked over at him. "You made some threats there, but will you carry them out?"

He smiled at her. "What do you think?"

"I want to know your thoughts on that, Conall."

"Absolutely. I have no problem telling you. If you hadn't been here, I would have taken them down myself," he shared, "but you'd already been hurt, and I wouldn't leave that to chance. Now, if you want to stay here, I'll go after them."

"No, I don't want you going after them," she cried out in horror.

"Somebody's got to stop them," he said, looking at her intently.

"Not you," she murmured. "That's what the sheriff and his deputies are for."

He looked at her and then rolled his eyes. "How much good have they been so far?"

She shook her head. "Not so much, but they can't all be lazy or bad."

"No, they can't, and they aren't. We had a bunch come out earlier," Conall noted, "but that doesn't mean they'll come out if they think we may be filing a complaint against God-only-knows who. Somebody in local law enforcement is clearly on the take or protecting someone, so we can't expect them to be fair to us."

"It's such a shit deal," she muttered, "and it's not fair to anybody."

"No, and that's why we have to make some waves."

Just then came a knock on the door. She stared at him, eyes wide, and he muttered, "The sheriff, remember?"

"*Great,*" she replied, "too little, too late."

"Yeah, but that's often the way." He walked over and opened the door to see two deputies standing there, glaring at him. He raised an eyebrow. "Now, if only you'd been like five minutes earlier, it might have done some good."

"We got a complaint from two citizens out in the parking lot that you pulled a gun on them."

He looked at them and then started to laugh. "Is that what the assholes said?"

The two men shook their heads. "They accused you of accosting them out in the parking lot. The complaint has named and described you very clearly."

Bethany stepped forward in a fit of rage, her face red and swollen. "And you believed them?" she asked in outrage.

They looked at each other, then at her and asked, "Will you tell us a different story?"

She glared at him, then shook her head. Turning to Conall, she said, "I guess talking to them won't do a damn bit of good, will it?"

The one officer replied, "Hey, that's not fair. We don't know what's going on, not until we hear the story from all sides."

She shook her head. "You don't give a crap about the story from my side," she snapped, glaring at them. She turned to Conall. "So much for Badger."

Just then Conall's phone vibrated. Taking it from his pocket, he spoke into the phone, testing to see if Badger was still listening in.

"About time you talked to me. I thought you had forgotten you were tying up my line."

Conall chuckled.

"Expect my guy soon." Then Badger disconnected.

A second pounding suddenly came on the door, and the vibrations alone might take the door off its hinges.

She glared at the two officers. "Do you mind moving, please?" She walked around them and opened the door. Another man stepped into the small apartment, looked at the two deputies, lifted his chin in acknowledgment, then turned to her and Conall, his gaze sharp. "Badger sent me."

Conall nodded. "Good, perfect timing. These officers were just explaining how someone accused us of attacking them at gunpoint and causing trouble for the local riffraff."

"Hey, hey, hey," the deputy added, "that's not fair."

"It's not untrue though, is it?" Conall added.

"We hadn't heard your side of the story yet."

"No, but you didn't exactly come in here asking for our story either," she snapped, glaring at them.

He just frowned, then looked over at his partner. "Seems we've missed something here."

His partner nodded. "Like we just stepped into the middle of something, to be honest."

"You did, but that's all right," Conall replied. "It's never too late to get on the right side."

"How do we know which is the right side?" he asked, looking from his partner back to the new arrival. "What did you mean about Badger sent you? Who the hell is Badger?"

He smiled. "Yeah, Badger sent me," he repeated cheerfully, "telling me how apparently there are some issues with local law enforcement."

"And who would you be?" one deputy asked.

He smiled bigger and held up a badge that Bethany couldn't see. Still she saw enough to see the color drain from the first deputy's face.

"Oh, good," Bethany said. "Anything that makes you guys leery must be a good thing for us."

"Now look. We just came because we got a complaint from a local citizen."

"Oh, that's interesting," she snapped, with a mock smile. "So, you didn't come in response to my phone call about intruders in my apartment. I'm a local too. And what about my report earlier about a gunman who attacked me at my place of business earlier today? It required additional calls by others," she added, glaring at the deputies.

The two uniformed men looked at each other and shook their heads. "We don't know anything about a report of an intruder, and I have to ask …" he began, stammering under the watchful gaze of the guy with the badge. "What are you involved in that has you ending up with gunmen in your place of work and your apartment today?"

She gasped, as she understood the hidden meaning in his words, but Conall reached out a hand and placed it on her shoulder. "Don't waste the energy." She spun on him, and he just smiled and pulled her into his chest. "You won't win an argument on this one, since it's to their advantage to assume you're the problem, and we aren't changing that right now."

Her shoulders slumped, and she turned to glare at the two deputies. "Officers, the door is behind you. Please use it."

"In that case, we'll have to take you in for questioning," the one deputy stated coolly, obviously not liking the way the conversation was going, "because you have been accused of harassment."

"Really? See this red mark on my face? Jake hit me. And I suppose that harassment complaint came from Jake too? Him and the local roughneck idiots associated with the family who owns the mill in town here, who basically supports your paycheck?" she snapped, with a knowing smile. "The very same riffraff who can come around with guns, beating people up and stealing from local businesses, doing whatever they like, and nobody lifts a finger to stop them?"

"That's not true," the one deputy countered stiffly, "and besides, we're just doing our jobs and following up on a complaint."

"I wonder where the complaint that I made went," she stated, glaring at him, "because it's obvious you're not here to help me."

At that, the new arrival motioned at the two deputies. "I would like to speak with you outside, please." They turned and glared at him, but he shrugged and added, "Or we can go down to the sheriff's office, your choice. On the other hand, I'll be going to see the sheriff in a little bit anyway, so don't worry about it."

"What's not to worry about?" the same deputy asked him.

"These two. I'll handle this issue, and, if you want them in for questioning, I'll bring them in with me," he replied smoothly. "It'll be you guys I want to talk to when I get there, so you've got"—he looked at his watch—"about forty-five minutes to get your stories straight."

"We don't answer to you," the one deputy snapped.

"No, you sure don't," he confirmed, with a cold smile, "but your boss will be calling you any minute now."

Just then, both of their phones went off. They looked at each other, quickly picked up their phones, and seeing who it was, they walked out.

At that, the new arrival turned to them and introduced himself. "My name's Greg."

"Glad to meet you," she said. "It's been a bit of a nightmare here."

"Sounds like it, and all over a War Dog." Greg smiled, as he turned to Conall. "You sure seem to be having some additional trouble."

"The War Dog brought me here," he stated, "but as I dislike misused authority ..."

"You and me both," Greg agreed cheerfully. "So, I need

a few more details. Badger didn't give me a whole lot to go on. He basically just told me to move my ass and to get here, so here I am." He looked from Conall to Bethany. "Now, give me a reason to go tear apart local law enforcement."

"Oh, you can have all of mine," she declared and launched into a long monologue about the three ruffians who stole free goods from the café all the time, then about Mel stealing the petty cash for Page, followed by Page copying her keys to enter her clinic to steal her drugs there, plus about Jake and his buddy who were just here, waving guns in their faces, and the smack that she had taken to her face.

When Greg heard that, he looked at her face, frowned, tilted it from side to side, and frowned. "We'll need to get photos of that."

She shrugged. "According to those deputies, Jake and his buddy were the ones making the complaint against me," she decided, "so it won't make a damn bit of difference."

"But I'm not them," Greg reminded her.

"Good enough," she muttered, but still she looked over at Conall. "Do you really think Greg will accomplish anything here?"

"He'll do what he can do," Conall said, "and we will take it from there."

She groaned. "Okay, fine. I'll let you take some pictures."

With that, Greg pulled out his phone and quickly took several photos of her face. "Now I need a timeline for when this all happened. And hopefully some idea of what it has to do with the War Dog."

She shook her head. "I don't know if it has anything to do with Bacchus," she admitted, turning to look at Conall.

"I'm not sure it does either," he agreed, with a shrug. "Except for the fact that, as soon as I got here, I got a good look at this town's underbelly. Me, an outsider. These punks have the locals all tight-lipped and doing what they say, but not me. So everything snowballed, and things got pretty rough." He then went into a tirade about what he had seen while here.

"So, nobody in law enforcement gives a crap?" Greg asked.

"Nope," Conall stated, "nobody seems to give a crap. You have a small town with ruffians running wild over the citizens, with no repercussions for their actions, and now we have a couple thieves in love who are stealing from various people, including a disabled veteran," he added, and he told him about Michael and the way the bank manager had reacted.

At that, Greg's face thinned, and he shook his head. "That will be a separate case," he stated. "There should never be that kind of elder abuse, particularly against any of our veterans."

"You and I both know they get targeted more than they should."

"They sure do," Greg muttered. He thought about it and added, "I definitely have something I can work with here. The question is whether I'll stop it or not."

"I don't know," Conall admitted. "I'm not sure exactly what it is that you do."

"One of the things I do," he shared, with a smirk, "is investigate law enforcement organizations and individuals who aren't doing their jobs. Generally citizen complaints get me called in," he explained, "which is why Badger gave me a shout."

"Interesting," Bethany muttered, staring at him. "I didn't even know there was such a thing."

"You can bet law enforcement doesn't like to let anybody know, and we don't interfere unless we have to," Greg stated, "but apparently, in this case, we need to."

"Yes," she snapped, "you do."

He chuckled, looked over at Conall. "Is she always this feisty, or just when she's riled?"

"I haven't known her all that long," Conall shared, with a smile, "but she does have good cause. It's her mother, Rosalind, who owns the diner, or co-owns it with Old Joe, I guess. That's where Jake and his crew keep going in and shaking them down, without paying. Interesting that they can be bothered doing petty stuff like that, but yet you said you have two separate cases here." Conall frowned at Greg.

"Yes, two separate cases, unless they dovetail now somehow," Greg stated, "and I won't be at all surprised if they do."

"You expect that to happen?" Bethany asked Conall.

CONALL FROWNED. "NOT really. I would have expected the young kids to leave town. These are the ones who stole from Michael, stole the petty cash from your business, then went back with copied keys, wielding a gun, shot at the floor in front of your feet." Conall faced Greg to include him more in this discussion. "Page already went back to Michael's place, and he chased him off, but Michael shouldn't be alone, which is why I've been staying there." Then he half smiled and faced Bethany again. "On the other hand, he may have a new romance brewing to keep him smiling through these next few difficult days."

"You're talking about Danny and his mom?" Bethany asked. "I never heard what all happened when you found the War Dog and everything."

He nodded. "Yes, apparently Michael and Mariam were sweethearts at one time, many years ago. Then, when he went off to war, she ended up staying behind and marrying somebody else."

"That would have been tough on him too," Greg noted. "That happened to a lot of blokes back then."

"It did, and that's a long time to wait for somebody," Bethany pointed out, turning to him. "I don't blame anybody for making decisions that they need to make."

"I don't either," Greg agreed, giving her half a smile. "It's more a case of whether something is here that we can use to make this a solid case or not."

"Tell me what you need from us or from the townsfolk," she said, "and I'll probably have lots of instances, maybe some witnesses or maybe not, but you should definitely talk to my mom about that too."

"I will," Greg stated, "and we need to talk to Michael."

At that, Conall nodded. "And soon too. I don't trust any of the punks around here at all."

Greg nodded. "I'll head over to talk to the sheriff and his staff members, and we will see what comes from that. I also want a copy of the report on what the ruffians outside accused you guys of doing because the minute a report is written up, we have to at least take a look at it," he explained, looking at Bethany apologetically.

"*Great,*" she muttered. "So, here I am, the innocent victim. I find that they've already burgled their way into my apartment. Then I get beaten up and threatened at gunpoint, not to mention scared half to death, and they put in a false report, and *we're* the ones who have to go in and justify what happened."

"Kind of sounds like that's why they did it, doesn't it?" Greg asked.

"Sure does. So, in other words, *what?* The cops are helping them? We already knew that," she declared, raising both hands in frustration.

"Maybe, but, if the local authorities are actively helping them dodge the law, then we have a whole lot more in terms of avenues to getting rid of them," Greg pointed out, smiling.

"Getting rid of which ones though?" she asked. "Are we looking at getting rid of the bad cops? Those punks? Page and Mel? Any or all would be lovely, yet, in the end, it won't make a damn bit of difference. They may shut down the mill because of that idiot son of his. Then people will lose their jobs, and that won't make anybody happy here either."

"Which is why the status quo exists," Greg stated. "That's why everybody will have to choose a side on this."

"I already chose mine," Bethany declared. "My mom lives in fear every time Jake and his thugs show up."

"That's no way to exist," Greg murmured, looking at her, "so let's do this."

"What do we need to do?" she asked.

"Come on down to the station with me. We already have your statement," he said, holding up his phone, "as I recorded it. We'll go down and listen to theirs, and hopefully we can make some headway."

"What more do you need?" she asked.

Looking at Conall, Greg asked, "Any chance at cameras?"

Conall smiled and nodded. "I saw cameras outside, so we should take a look at those."

"Good." Then Greg asked Conall, "Why did you come inside, if you thought they were in here? I can't understand why would you come in?"

"I asked him not to," Bethany said glumly, "but he wouldn't let the riffraff ruin my life any more than it already was—or something to that effect."

Conall laughed. "Sometimes it's just better to face bullies head-on," he stated, "but, before we headed inside, Jake came up behind us with a gun and escorted us inside." Then he reached over and stroked her cheek, "All of that aside, I wish I could have stopped him from hitting you."

"What about you?" she said, turning and looking at him. "He dropped you to the ground."

He smiled and nodded. "He did, and I owe him one for that, but it's also a whole lot easier to drop and roll and take the blow, so they think I'm a cripple after all."

"Did he hurt you?" Greg asked, turning to look at him.

He shrugged. "Nope, I'm fine."

Bethany added, "He wears a prosthetic, and these guys knew it. So that was their idea of taking advantage."

Immediately Greg looked at Conall's leg and asked, "Don't suppose that's one of Kat's, is it?"

"Sure it is," Conall confirmed, with a smile, "and believe me, I'm blessed to have it."

"Damn, it would almost be worth losing a leg to get one of her fancy designs. Sorry, I know that's probably insulting, but I find her abilities fascinating."

"Oh, I get it, and look. I'm just wearing the plain-Jane model," he said, lifting his pant leg. "I'm hoping to get a fancy dress unit eventually, but we're not there yet. Kat has to fix the knee joint first. It isn't quite there yet."

"She doesn't charge you guys full cost either, does she?"

"She charges something for her time and the materials, but it's unbelievable how many hours she really puts in. Even afterward, she doesn't treat it like a final product to be sold, nor does she treat it like a full custom job, and yet it is," Conall explained, with a shrug. "Honestly they must be pretty well off to even begin to do what they're doing, yet kind enough to see it all through."

"Yeah, that would be Kat," Greg noted in a reminiscent tone. "I've known her a long time."

"I'm glad you were there to take her and Badger's call," Bethany stated. "We obviously need all the help we can get."

"Oh, it'll all come out in the wash," Greg promised, with a smile. "You would be amazed what can happen when somebody from my department shows up."

She looked over at him and smiled. "I'm really glad you're here to deal with the bullies."

His eyebrows shot up, and he looked over at Conall, who chuckled. "Honey, he's not here to deal with the bullies," he clarified. "Greg's here to patch up the law enforcement."

"Oh." She stared at Greg, yet asked Conall, "He can't do both?"

Conall replied, "To a certain extent, he can help with one or the other, but his real purpose for being here is to look at law enforcement who's not doing its job."

"Right." She winced. "That means we'll have to deal with the bullies."

"Yep, it sure does," Conall said cheerfully, "and I, for one, can't wait."

# CHAPTER 12

Conall drove Bethany to the nearest sheriff's office, with Greg going in his own vehicle. When they arrived, Greg had already entered the building. Conall parked, and they both exited his truck. He reached out a hand, and she immediately reached back.

Taking a deep breath, she shook her head. "I really don't want to go in there."

"I know," he replied, "and it appears we're up against some serious heavy hitters. There's an interesting chaos with the extra players and issues and all that. But the thing to remember is that you've done nothing wrong and that you need to stay calm." When she shot him a look, he smiled. "I know. Asking you to stay calm about this issue is not an easy thing."

"Not only is it *not* easy," she declared, "it's ridiculous. I mean, I come home after a day from hell at my business, only to find people in my apartment, and, before I know it, someone is waving a weapon in my face, hitting me, and threatening me. Then they go outside and tell the deputies a completely different story, and the authorities believed *them*."

Conall clarified, "The deputies believed them *so far*, but that doesn't mean they'll continue to believe them or that they'll continue to be inactive over all this."

"Yet you and I both know we're up against some longstanding trouble."

He held up a hand. "We can't know everything. Let's just go see how far the sheriff is willing to go to protect these guys. After that, we'll have a talk, or somebody will. It seems as if maybe somebody is acting as the old guard, who appears to be bankrolling whatever these guys want to do."

"What are the chances," she asked, "and I know this is probably very unlikely, … but what are the chances that whoever that is doesn't even know what these armed bullies are really up to, since everybody keeps letting them get away with it?"

"That would be a very interesting question to ask," he noted, "because we're assuming that Jake's dad or someone is allowing all this to happen, but what if he doesn't have a clue?"

She nodded. "I had a pretty laid-back dad but I was young so never really got into serious trouble. Of course I didn't really get into trouble until a teenager then, oh, boy, I really got into trouble." She laughed. "However, I never pulled anything anywhere close to the shit these kids are pulling."

"Of course not," Conall agreed. "This is way too many steps too far."

"They'll say I have no proof, right?"

"No proof of what?" he asked, looking at her.

"No proof that they hit me and no proof of the gun because these thugs won't show up at the sheriff's department with it."

"You have my witness statement too. Yet that's an interesting point, and one that I'm damn sure that they would refute. Do you have any security cameras at your place?"

She nodded and brought it up on her phone.

"Replay it back. Why do you have cameras at home?" he asked.

"Mostly because I live alone," she explained. "I didn't do anything about the lock on the front door, which I now see that I should have," she admitted, with an eye roll. "Still I do have security cameras in place, … just in case."

She brought it up on her phone, and there was a picture of her front door. "Oh, my God. Why didn't I think of this before? I should have showed Greg."

"You can show Greg when we go inside. It's even better this way."

The two of them stepped closer, reviewing the video, as they watched their two gunmen break through her door, picking the lock, and going inside, with big grins on their faces. They searched her place. Then they moved in and out range of the cameras, but their guns were obvious.

Conall asked, "You don't shut off the cameras, do you?"

"No, I don't," she said. "I generally just ignore them. I don't even know when I last looked at any footage. Since I have just the two cameras, and both face the front door, it's not a big issue for me."

Sure enough, they continued watching. The camera showed the two of them coming in with one of the gunmen behind them, waving a gun.

"That just proves they were in your apartment and that they were waving a gun," Conall said. Outside of the visuals caught on the frame, there was no sound. So unfortunately Bethany getting slapped was not heard, but the camera caught Bethany when she staggered back from being hit. Conall's jaw clenched as he relived her getting slapped. On camera, he could just see her arm and body swing low, and then she slowly straightened up.

The camera didn't catch Conall getting knocked to the ground, which was neither here nor there. For him, it was all about her being attacked. "Can you send that to me?"

"Yeah, if I can figure out how," she muttered. She swiped her phone screen several times and then sent him a copy.

"I'm sending this to Badger too," he murmured.

"Can Badger really do anything about it?"

"He'll be interested in seeing what ends up happening, especially now, since we have actual video proof," he noted, a bit pleased. "That is huge."

"I often thought I was stupid to have that system."

"It's sad that you have to have it," he noted, "but it's definitely not stupid. It's only stupid when you *don't* have it and wish you did. … That's the regret most people usually have."

They walked into the sheriff's office soon afterward. Conall headed to Greg and asked, "What's your email address?" Greg gave it to him, and Conall quickly forwarded the video to him as well.

When it popped up in his email, Greg pulled out his phone, clicked on the video, and watched. He nodded at the two of them with a knowing smile. "Really glad you've got that."

"Yeah, me too," she said. "Sorry, I hadn't even thought about it when we were all there. I was a little stressed," she admitted, shooting a glance around at the others.

And, of course, her tormenters were here, the two who had been in her apartment. Jake's dad was here too. She studied the older man, who was pacing the station hallway, talking on the phone. "So, that's Jake's father? Is he calling a lawyer?" she asked Greg.

"Yes, Henry is Jake's father. He's on some sort of business call," Greg shared.

"Ah, so this doesn't even warrant a lawyer, right? I mean, his son is the supposed injured party here."

"That's what the supposed injured party is saying, yes." Greg smiled.

The sheriff, at that point in time, walked over to see them. She glanced up at him and gave him a curt nod.

"I hear you're causing trouble," he began, with a genuine smile. "I'm hoping we can settle this nicely."

"Yeah, I hope so too," she declared, "but I can assure you that I'm not the one who's causing trouble."

His smile slowly disappeared. He looked back at Greg and then over at Conall. "You guys will cause trouble, won't you?" he asked, with a resigned chuckle.

"I don't know about *causing trouble*," she spat, "but how do you feel about people breaking into apartments, wielding weapons, and attacking women just trying to come home from work?"

The smile slowly dropped off his face. "Of course you can't prove that, and you do realize there are harassment allegations against you."

She glanced over at Greg, and he explained, "We have a video you should see," he replied, as he walked over to one of the boardroom tables, found a projector, and quickly connected the SD card from his phone.

Within seconds, the video was playing on a full screen inside the boardroom, where everybody out in the lobby could also see it, since the interior windows into that boardroom were all open, instead of curtained for privacy.

Greg put it on Replay, and it just cycled over and over

again, until everybody, standing inside or outside the room, watched the recording from start to finish. Henry stepped into the open doorway and watched the video in its entirety. The anger on his face was something to behold.

Bethany watched it build with apprehension and a bit of delight, wondering whether Henry finally understood what his son had been doing, or was just angry that Jake had been caught?

As soon as Jake saw what his father was watching, Jake raced over. "Dad, I can explain."

Henry turned to him, and the look on his face was something that made even Bethany cringe.

Jake backed up. "Honest, I can explain."

"You can explain this?" his father asked in a deathly low voice. "You can explain how you broke into a woman's apartment and did all this with a weapon clearly on display, then lied to the sheriff about it?"

"Dad—"

"You've lied to *me* about it too," Henry added, staring at his son as if he didn't have a clue who he was. "I see now that you've been lying to me all this time. About how everybody has been treating you so badly. About how you were being picked on because you were my son and about how life was so difficult here that you wanted help to get away to go do something else with your life because this was so tough?" He stared directly at his son.

"Instead, I find out that *you* are the bully, that you're the one who's been doing all this crap and God-only-knows what else, including beating up innocent women." He clearly still felt a sense of shock. "What the hell, Jake."

He continued to stare at his son, and you could almost see that, between them, a whole new awareness was happening. Henry clearly had not the slightest idea what the son had really been up to.

Jake shook his head, looking frantic. "No, you don't understand. I finally just hit a wall. I couldn't take it anymore. She's been just terrible."

"*She*? *She* has been terrible?" His father just looked at him, his gaze never once breaking. "All this time I've been protecting you. All this time I've been helping you with all this trouble you've gotten into because I felt sorry for you." He frowned at Jake. "I felt guilty because my role in the community was causing you these problems. And now here we have video proof of what you've really been doing."

"That video doesn't show anything," Jake burst out. "It doesn't show anything."

At that, Jake's dad turned to the sheriff, cutting off the tirade of his son, and said, "My apologies, Sheriff. Obviously I need to take my son home and have a *talk* with him. I can assure you that this sort of thing won't happen again." He turned to his son, motioned toward the door, and said, "Move it."

Jake shook his head.

"Go," he snapped. "We'll talk about this at home." Henry looked at everybody else and said, "My deepest apologies for any trouble my son has caused."

As he headed to the door, Conall called out, "That's not enough, sir."

The man froze, then turned and looked at him with a wary expression. "What are you talking about? I've apologized."

"*You* have apologized, and that's nice and all," Conall replied, waving his hand. "However, your son hasn't. Jake is still denying how he attacked this woman, striking her in the face, knocking her to the ground, after breaking into her apartment and wielding a gun in her face. Those are criminal offenses, and Bethany will press charges, and I will be her witness, along with that security tape footage and our written statements," Conall declared, staring at Jake's dad with a hard glare. "Your son does not get a free pass on this."

Henry faced the sheriff, his gaze intense as he spoke. "This is a first offense, so my son should be allowed a second chance."

Conall shook his head. "With all due respect, sir, your son is a hoodlum who has been causing chaos in this town, completely free of any accountability for his actions," Conall added, not backing down one inch. "He steals from the coffee shop owners—threatening them if they demand payment for Jake's crew's coffee or the lunches that he orders from them. He has made everybody in that town afraid because that's what he does. He bullies and intimidates to get what he wants, all because he knows that you will protect him."

At that, Henry stiffened and glared. "And who are you?"

"Nobody to you," Conall stated, "but I am somebody who will matter to your son because I will not rest until he faces jail time for these crimes."

Jake snorted. "My dad can fix this."

"Yes, your dad probably can fix this," Conall agreed. "Of course he can make other things blow up really, really quickly too, but he might not like the end result, considering that we are also assessing the actions of the Sheriff's Office in this matter. Maybe your dad shouldn't fix this. Since he has now seen proof that you've been lying and misrepresenting things, maybe Henry won't want to be known as the man who protected his son from charges of assaulting an innocent woman in her home, while holding her at gunpoint. What's next for you, Jake? Murder? Where do you stop?"

"That's enough—" Jake began.

"Agreed," Conall said. "That's my point exactly, Jake. Enough is enough. You haven't stopped yet, and you're just running this town on sheer … shoddiness," he determined, after trying to come up with a better word and failing.

The kid snorted. "You don't even know English," he muttered.

"And you do?" Conall asked him, raising an eyebrow. "Do you understand what *criminal charges* mean?"

"You can't charge me with anything," he snapped. "I've only done this stuff in this county, and nobody spoke up because it's not a big deal."

Conall raised an eyebrow at Greg, who stared at Jake with interest. "Oh, so you do understand parts of the law, and you intentionally kept all your criminal activities within the boundaries of the location where your father could bail you out. Is that it?"

Jake shrugged. "I'm not stupid."

"Yet you are stupid," his father snapped, as he turned and glared at him. "Now shut your mouth, and we'll go home and talk about this."

"You won't be taking him anywhere just yet," Greg said, with a lazy smile.

Henry turned to his buddy. "Sheriff?"

The sheriff blustered, his gaze going to the others in the room, and then he frowned at the older man. "Look, Henry. You've got to understand. Jake has really crossed the line this time. He beat up a woman in her own apartment, while wielding a firearm. And it's all on video."

Henry paled. "*Striking a blow* now graduating to *beating*

*up* seems like an exaggeration."

"Really?" Bethany snapped, as she stepped forward. "An exaggeration, really? So, the fact that I was struck and that Conall was struck down doesn't matter? Does that make it any worse in your eyes, or, because Conall's a male, it doesn't matter? Or perhaps because I, the woman, was only struck once, it doesn't really matter either? What are you, a wife-beater yourself?" she snapped, as she glared at Henry. "Is one blow allowed, but two is too much? Is that how you determine the right and wrong in this instance?"

Henry glanced around the room, and his face had turned all shades of red and purple.

"You have protected him the entire time he's been running free in this county, absolutely destroying any sense of decency that our town once had, killing its economy too. And, let me remind you, it is *my mother* he keeps threatening at the cafe," she added, glaring at Jake.

Henry looked back at the kid, assessing the situation, but there was more to come from Bethany.

She was not done yet.

"He hasn't paid for any food or drink in the café for so long that it's ridiculous. He obnoxiously orders things they don't offer, then loudly berates and threatens them. If we had realized your son was so broke, people might have taken pity on him and offered him a meal."

Henry stiffened at that. Turning, he frowned at his son. "Are you telling me that you've run up a bill that you can't afford to pay?"

"Run up a bill?" Conall repeated in a mocking tone. "He barges in, rude as hell, then gets what he ordered, walks out without paying, tossing a threat or two behind him. And it's not just him but his lovely little gang of goons as well."

Henry glared at Jake, shaking his head. "Seriously? You don't have any money to pay?"

"Oh, he has the money to pay," Bethany replied. "If he has money to buy guns, surely he could pay for his food. Yet he chooses *not* to pay, as you well know, because this is not the first you've heard about it, and there is no use pretending it is."

Henry turned back to look at Bethany. "I don't like your attitude."

"I don't like yours either," she spat. "Just because you own the mill that employs a lot of the people here, that does not allow you to run roughshod over them and us, as if you're not subject to the same rules of a civilized community as the rest of us, but you are. I just trust that some authority curtails the abuses you and your son have subjected us all to."

"My abuses?" Henry asked, staring at her in shock.

"You have been protecting this maniac," she snapped. "He needs to be held accountable for what he's done. And he needs to know that you can't and won't bail him out anymore."

"That's not fair," Jake snapped. "I hardly even touched you."

"You did attack me, at gunpoint, and you did much more than *barely touch me*," she declared, turning to glare at him. "You knocked me to the ground and threatened me. You also knocked Conall to the ground, all because you wanted to show what a big man you were, but you're not a big man at all," she snapped. "You're nothing but a little boy, hiding behind a gun and your dad's bank balance."

That was it, and Jake went from zero to sixty, instantly lunging at her, knocking her over and landing on top of her.

Conall was there in an instant, picking up Jake and easily tossing him across the room. Everybody else froze in position. "This is your son," Conall yelled, turning to look at Jake's father. "Has he made you proud yet, or is there more you want to see? This is who he is—uncontrolled, driven by power and ego, none of which he has earned." Conall obviously still struggled to hold back his temper. "Too scared to take on his physical equals, Jake attacks women and the elderly, his favorite targets, who are afraid to report him because of his threats."

Jake added, "You're nothing but a cripple, an easy target."

"Cripple, *huh*? How do you figure?"

"I figured, if I picked on you, you would have whined and said you were some sort of injured veteran or something," he explained, with a sneer, "just like that old man in the wheelchair."

"Are you talking about Michael Stanford?" Jake's father asked, his tone deepening. "Michael served in the military and deserves our respect."

"Oh, cut the crap, Dad. You don't believe that bullshit. Just because Granddad and your brother died in the war doesn't mean you give a crap. You're just saying that to make yourself look good, but you don't mean it."

Henry shook his head. "Dear God," he muttered, looking as if in shock, unless it was all for show. "What happened to you, Jake?"

"Nothing happened to me," Jake declared, glaring at his father. "Come on. Fix this shit, and let's go home. I'm hungry."

His father sagged into the closest chair and just stared at him, until he looked over at Conall, then the sheriff, and asked, "It won't fix so easily this time, will it?"

"Particularly not after that little public display here, no," the sheriff replied uneasily, as he looked around. "I can't fix everything, Henry."

Jake's father nodded sadly. "No, I can see that, and I can also see that I've allowed myself to be blind."

At that, Bethany snorted again.

He glared at her, then shrugged. "Okay, you have reason to hold something against Jake. I'll admit that his behavior just now was a little upsetting."

"*A little upsetting?*" she snapped. "I've now been physically attacked by your son twice, and you're a *little upset?* What about me? Did it occur to anyone but Conall to see if I was injured?"

"He looks like he's perfectly capable of handling anything that might happen to you," Henry replied, as he stared at his son thoughtfully. "I'm just not exactly sure what I'm supposed to do from here."

"What you're supposed to do from here is ensure Jake goes to jail and learns his lesson," Conall replied. "That will depend on if you're man enough to do that."

Henry just stared at him, then finally relented. "I suppose you're a veteran too, aren't you?"

"I sure am," he stated proudly, "and you can bet that, had your son served in the military"—he gave Jake a smirk—"he might have gotten some discipline and learned the value of a day's work, something I don't think he's ever done before."

"No, he hasn't," Henry admitted. "I had such a rough upbringing myself, after losing my father at such a young age, that I was determined to see that my son had a much better life."

"Do you think he's had a better life now? So you think Jake's *better life* comes at the cost of others having a shitty life?" Conall asked, as he walked over to stand in front of Henry. "Jake has zero respect for anyone. He only believes in his own ego and his own power, which is really only *your* power, because all you've ever done is protect him."

Henry shook his head. "Shit," he muttered, as he rubbed his face. "It's a good thing your mother's not here right now, Jake."

At that, the kid snorted. "Come on, Dad. You're not really listening to these guys, are you? They're just lying and making all this up."

"Are they?" Henry asked, looking at his son, with a sad look on his face. "Are they really, Jake?"

"Of course they are," Jake replied, the first note of alarm evident in his tone. "You can hear it yourself. You don't believe any of the shit they're talking about."

"I just saw you completely lose your temper and attack her, and not only attack her but you made no apology and showed no regret for what you did," Henry explained, looking at him. "That alone makes the rest of their story, such as how you've behaved at the diner, seem quite plausible. What am I supposed to do with that?"

"You ignore it," Jake snapped, glaring at him. "Come on. Let's go home and have a couple beers."

His father frowned. "Is that what you think will happen? A couple beers and this will all go away?"

"Sure, you just need to tell the sheriff to make it go away, like you always do."

"*Like I always do,*" Henry muttered sadly, as he looked over at the others. "My apologies. I hadn't realized it was as bad as all this."

"Of course not," Conall noted. "We don't always want to wake up to see what's in front of us."

"No, … we don't, but I still don't quite understand what I'm supposed to do at this point."

"Nothing *you* can do," Greg declared, as he stepped forward. "I'm here to make sure this situation is handled lawfully, so there will be no talking Jake's way out of this one."

"And yet it's his first offense," Henry repeated.

"No, it's not. It's his first offense that will be on the books because you've protected him. It's not his first offense by far, and believe me—by the time I finish my investigation and interview the rest of the townsfolk whom Jake has been terrorizing—there will be nothing left to discuss."

Henry looked over at his son with a genuine sadness. "Damn, Jake, what a waste."

For the first time, Jake started to look nervous. "What? Hang on a minute. Hang on. What are we talking about here?"

"We're talking about you paying for your actions," Conall said, looking at him in disgust. "Then maybe, for once, you'll understand how wrong you've been."

"I don't give a shit what you say," he spat, staring at Conall. "You're nothing but a fucking cripple. Just get the hell out of here and take that bitch with you."

"Why? So you don't feel aggravated enough to attack her again?" Conall asked in a jeering tone, thinking he wouldn't mind in the least if Jake jumped him.

"Look. Don't even talk to me. In fact, just seeing you makes me sick," Jake snapped, sneering in Conall's face. "I don't know what's wrong with her that she would even want to be with you, but it's just gross. You're wearing a prosthetic or something. You take off a body part? That's just disgusting, man."

His father stared at him sharply. "Stop it, Jake. Not another word!"

"Stop what? You don't believe this guy gives a shit about anything, do you? Come on, Dad. You're not that stupid, are you?"

His father just stared at him, as if he didn't understand what could possibly have triggered that kind of response. Yet, when he looked at the others, he saw the same understanding of what was going on that he had missed all these years. "Damn." Henry looked over at the sheriff. "Is there anything you can do?"

"I don't know," the sheriff admitted. "I can tell you this, Henry. … My job's on the line here, as I'll be investigated for all I've done up to now. There's still the question of hassling the locals," he noted, wincing. "It was one thing to keep him in control, but he really is ripping off the stores. He walks in, takes what he wants, and walks out. It's not just the café, but the corner store and other places too."

Henry closed his eyes and rubbed his temples. "Oh, my God," he muttered, eyeing his son. "You get thousands of dollars every month for spending money."

"Yeah? So what? Why would I spend it on that stuff when I don't have to? No fun in that, and, besides, there are better things to spend it on."

"What are you spending it on?" Henry asked, looking at him closely.

Jake shrugged. "Stuff."

"No, that's not good enough. What stuff?"

Jake glared at his father. "I don't know, just stuff."

"I hear drugs are expensive," Conall suggested.

Jake spun on a dime and glared at him. "I'm not into any goddamn drugs, and don't you be telling my father any more lies. Just keep your trap shut."

"I don't have to tell your father any lies, Jake. Your father can see for himself that you're lying, now that he's looking for the truth. Drug abuse is what I smell on you. And abusing women? Do you beat them up too?"

He shook his head. "I don't have to beat up women. They're quite happy to be with me."

"Are they?" Bethany asked, a serious look on her face. "I highly doubt that. What's going on? You're buying drugs for them or threatening to go to their parents over the drugs or whatever way you're using to get them into your bed," she snapped. "No way they would go willingly."

He took two steps toward her, and his father immediately stood, but it was Conall who stepped right in front of her, as he motioned at Jake. "Come on at me. Just one more step," Conall taunted. "You touch her one more time, and I will not hold back."

"Yeah, and what will you do, you freaking loser?" Jake bellowed. "I can kick that leg out from under you, and you would be on the ground, begging for mercy."

"Try it," Conall said, as he stared at him. He waited.

"Don't you dare," Henry muttered. "He's just egging you on."

"How come he's allowed to do that? I can't have that lack of respect. You know that, Dad. You taught me that respect is everything."

Conall snorted. "Did your father tell you that respect is earned and not bought? Maybe you forgot to give him that lesson," Conall slyly told Henry.

Henry turned to look at the sheriff. "Look. While you

sort out what you need to do, can I take him home and at least have a talk with him? If I can get the truth out of him about everything he's been involved in, I can figure out some sort of restitution."

The sheriff hesitated, then finally said, "You go ahead home, Henry, but Jake's not allowed to leave. I'll be coming by later to see you."

"With what? Charges? I don't think so," Jake sneered. "Ain't no way you'll charge me with anything."

Conall smiled and said, "If nobody else does, rest assured that I will." And he walked over to block the front door.

"Move," Jake snorted, walking toward the door to leave. The kid stopped, looked back at his dad, then faced Conall. "I don't think so, cripple. You see? My dad's a badass, and he'll make damn sure that nobody touches me," he muttered. "Especially not a cripple like you."

"Yeah? You're just too scared to do your own dirty work," Conall taunted him again, with a big smile, widening his stance at the front door. "You've been hiding behind your daddy for so long you don't even know what it's like to not be his pet."

His father immediately faced Jake and shook his head. "Don't even think about it."

"I won't allow such disrespect," Jake yelled madly. "My name is all about respect." He glared at his father. "I carved respect out of the damn town, just like you did, and no way in hell I'll let this piece of shit talk to me like that." He turned to Conall. "I said … move."

Conall remained blocking the door. As Henry headed toward the door now too, Conall remained standing right there before him.

Jake smiled and muttered, "This is perfect." Then pulling out a gun, he pointed at Conall and fired.

# CHAPTER 13

BETHANY FROZE IN shock as Conall went down, only to bounce back up again, his leg kicking out hard and fast, dropping the smirking Jake, kicking the gun free to skitter across the floor, as every other man in room the raced toward Jake. Bethany couldn't believe Jake had shot Conall. As soon as Jake was subdued, she raced over to Conall. "Are you okay?" she cried out.

He nodded. "I'm fine, no thanks to this punk." He looked over at Henry. "What now? You still think Jake should be let off? What'll it take to get your attention?"

Henry's hand was over his mouth, as he stared at the remnants of his faith in his son. "Dear God, what the hell happened to him?"

"What happened is his belief that he is untouchable," Bethany explained, looking over at Henry. "The belief that his daddy will get him out of everything, supported by the knowledge that you always have."

Henry shook his head, as he stared at her. "What did I do that was so wrong? I was just trying to protect my son, to give him a better life."

"But what you did was create a monster, with no accountability for his actions," she whispered.

Even now Jake glared at the sheriff, who struggled to restrain him.

"It's not like you can fucking contain me," Jake yelled. "Dad, you want to call him off?"

Jake's bored tone had his father gawking at him in horror. "*Call him off?* You just shot somebody in the police station," he cried out. "Not only is that absolutely insane, it's the stupidest location you could possibly have thought of."

Bethany turned and glared at him. "Shit like that is what you're doing wrong."

"What?" Henry asked.

"You basically just told Jake that it was okay to do what he did but next time choose a better location."

"No, I didn't mean it that way," Henry replied, staring at her, then looking back at his son. "Obviously it's stupid to shoot anybody."

But Jake was laughing. "That's okay, Dad. I got the right message." He glared at the others. "Obviously the cripple's not hurt, so no repercussions are needed here," Jake declared, shrugging the men off, trying to restrain him.

They let him go, even as she watched in surprise. "Why are you not locking him up?" she asked, turning to the sheriff.

The sheriff motioned to another room. "Put him in the interrogation room. Things are obviously very heated now."

She stared. "Did you say, *very heated?* Jake just shot Conall right in front of you."

"Settle down," the sheriff snapped at her. "Obviously this is a spurious accusation."

Greg stepped forward, and, in an overly calm voice, he asked, "*Spurious accusation?* Sheriff, are you suggesting that there weren't a half-dozen witnesses to Jake's attempted murder?"

The sheriff winced. "Okay, okay, so maybe that wasn't

the right choice of words," he clarified in an uncertain tone. "Everybody just calm down. This is my office, and I'll handle this how I see fit."

Greg stared at him for a moment, then shook his head. "No, Sheriff. You'll handle it by the law, or you'll be out of a job. And possibly facing charges of your own."

In the ensuing silence, the sheriff just stared at him.

Greg smiled. "Sheriff, do you really think that people from my division come here on the basis of one problem?" As the sheriff began to turn pale, Greg continued. "Do you think other people in this county haven't made complaints because you weren't doing anything about this? Now that I've seen it for myself, it's far worse than we imagined."

Bethany turned and looked at Conall, still amazed that he was unhurt. "How did he miss at that range?"

He gave her half a laugh. "While it was a piss-poor shot, it's not that he missed as much as he hit my prosthetic. Kat will be pretty upset." He bent down and lifted his pant leg for her to see the hole.

She stared at it in shock. "So, it hit you?"

"He did hit me," he confirmed, "and you can bet that will be on the report."

"He said he missed."

"Jake *thought* he missed, and honestly it could have been a good shot because I don't know whether this will impact the workability of my joint or not," he shared, frowning, as he stared down at his prosthetic.

"I'm so sorry," she whispered. "I never intended for that to happen."

Conall shook his head. "It has nothing to do with you. This is not your fault."

She gave him a sad gaze. "Yes, it is."

"No, it's not," he repeated, staring at her. "You can't let bullies like him keep running the town, and you know that as well as I do. I was just the right person at the right time to lend a hand."

"But what happens when you leave?" she asked, looking around. "You know that the sheriff will buckle, as will Henry, and Jake will be out on the streets in no time, and I'll become the next target."

"I think Greg will be changing Jake's location to a different holding facility. Plus I'm not planning on leaving anytime soon," Conall shared. "Besides, we still have another pair of hoodlums to deal with."

She winced. "Melanie and Page, Michael's nephew."

He nodded. "That won't be easy either. You know that."

"I do know," she admitted. "I was hoping we could just get a pass." The words had no sooner left her mouth, when Greg came over.

He bent closer to Conall and asked in a low voice, "How badly damaged is your prosthetic?"

"I don't know for sure," he admitted, shaking his head. "It just pisses me off that he did it in the first place."

"Do you think it was on purpose?" Greg asked.

Conall snorted, then shrugged. "I wouldn't be at all surprised. Jake will believe that it isn't important, but I think he's more directed in his actions than we think."

"What'll be the end result here?" Bethany asked.

Greg replied, "Monetary damages are due to Conall, besides the threat of death. The sheriff can't let that go," Greg explained. "So it'll be interesting to see what he says, but I'm staying here to make sure that this gets handled appropriately."

She nodded.

Henry was still trying to absorb what had happened to his life and to his son.

She walked over and spoke to Henry. "At this point, you should consider it a kindness to let him face his own consequences to make him grow up now. If he continues on this path, he'll get himself killed."

He looked up at her. "I don't even know how to stop him at this point," he shared, his tone low. "I understand what you mean, but nobody here will shoot him."

"He already held a gun to me and has now shot Conall once. Do you expect a man like Conall to take it lying down, should your son try it again?"

He stared at her, then looked back at Conall and winced. "Unfortunately he does look like the kind of man to do the job."

"He could, particularly if *I* was attacked again," she pointed out. "There are very few things in life that these men will fight for so strongly, but women getting beaten up is definitely one of them."

Henry sighed and nodded. "As it should be." He looked back at the son he'd raised on his own. "You spend all that time raising them, thinking that you're doing a good job. And sure, I stepped in and protected him a couple times, but I didn't realize what that was doing to him."

"It gave him free rein," she said softly, "and he's taken full advantage of it."

"Which I don't even know what to do with," he said, staring at her in despair. "He's my only child."

"If you want him to survive, he needs to grow up, and he needs to grow up fast," she stated. "Honestly I don't have any sympathy for him. If he continues pulling guns on people, it won't end well. He'll wind up in prison for life, or worse, and, while I would be sad for you and for the simple waste of human life gone bad, I can't say I would feel badly for Jake because, frankly, he deserves whatever he gets at this point. I'm happy he's on the warpath right now in front of you and the authorities, and I'm hoping you let Jake think about it in jail, and you don't bail him out."

Henry winced. "Bail is something that every criminal gets," he argued, "so, of course, I'll bail him out."

"But you also know that he will likely break bond and come after me and Conall."

He stared at her. "You could always leave town."

"So, *we're* supposed to leave town? … How does that make sense? I run a veterinarian business," she stated, staring at him. "So I'm supposed to give up everything so that your hoodlum son doesn't get into more trouble, is that it?"

His shoulders sagged, and he whispered, "Before today that would have definitely been it, so I guess that's where the problem started."

"That's *exactly* where the problem started," she declared, shaking her head. "I have a right to my life too, not to just be caught up in Jake's moods whenever he takes a notion to cause chaos and to steal and to abuse women."

"Has he really been going to the cafe and taking whatever he wants?"

She nodded. "Usually a burger, coffee, some pies, anything he can get away with, never too big, never such that it's massive, and all he's taking is meals. But it's just getting worse all the time, like he's escalating, as are his threats," she explained. "We had no idea he had a weapon, but now that he does or did," she stated, "that's even more troublesome."

Henry sighed, raising both hands. "We have lots of weapons at home, so, even if he doesn't get this one back, he'll just go to the gun cabinet and get another."

She stared at him, her stomach sinking. "*Thanks* for that," she spat. "I'm sure I won't sleep again."

He looked at her and frowned. "I'm sorry he hit you."

"Yeah, but will you be sorry when he tries to kill me?" she asked bluntly. "Because I think you're still looking to protect your son."

"That's just it. He is my son." Henry stared at her. "How come you don't understand that?"

"I guess because I would like to think that my life or the lives of the others he threatens have some value too. But, to you, it seems absolutely nothing else is of value, except your son, and that's sad, Henry. It's sad because other people in this world have a right to a good life, without being terrorized by Jake and his goons, and you can't see that. That's where the problem is. You must realize that Jake and his hoodlum friends are running people out of town, that the town itself is dying because of Jake?"

Henry hesitated, shaking his head.

"So, here's hoping your son doesn't get released on bail," she stated, tossing him a look. "And maybe, just maybe, that way he won't get himself killed or wind up in prison."

"I heard that," Jake roared from the other room. "Don't you talk to my dad like that."

"Yeah? Or what?" she asked from the doorway. "Will you come after me again? Will you shoot me now?"

"I just might," he threatened in a hard voice. "You don't get to treat him like that."

"Right, you guys are both messed up in the head," she muttered, as she walked closer to Conall. "Can we leave now?"

He looked over at the sheriff. "I'm sure the sheriff would

be more than happy if we disappeared. You ready to go?"

"I was ready to go before we even got here," she muttered, as she glanced over at Greg. "We'll head back to my place, if you need us. We're tired and worn out, and this has definitely screwed up my emotions."

Greg nodded. "Just stay safe, please."

She froze at that. "Is Jake likely to get out?"

"If he makes bail, yes." Greg waved his hands about. "There's a lot of paperwork to handle first, but I can't stop him from getting bail."

"Even if he's a danger to somebody else?"

"There's no judge in town, and that's often one of the reasons to let them go home and stay, at least until the judge shows up. In this case, it shouldn't happen, since Jake's fired a weapon in the sheriff's office for all to see. He should be locked up and the key thrown away, but you and I both know it won't go that way."

"You can't stop it?" Bethany asked in horror.

"The question is whether I *should* stop it," he replied, looking over at her, "or do I need the sheriff to hang himself a little more by releasing Jake?"

She thought about that and nodded. "I guess, in the end, that would probably be the better idea, ... but that doesn't mean I like it."

"Of course not," Greg agreed, with a smile, "but you will have Conall with you though."

"Yes," she muttered, "but he also took a bullet in that joint. He's not even sure if the joint will work, and that's something else to consider."

He nodded. "I'll stop by in a little bit, if you want."

She looked down at her watch and said, "Make it tomorrow. I need to get some sleep in a big way."

"Got it." Greg smiled. "If it's not very late, I'll send you guys a text to confirm everything is okay with you."

And, with that, she walked over to Conall. "Come on. Let's go home."

"Where's home?" he asked, looking at her with interest. "That could be over at Michael's, or it could be at your place."

"It needs to be at my place," she stated, shaking her head. "I won't sleep if I'm alone there tonight."

"Ah." He nodded. "That is a very valid point, but it kind of sucks though. This is what we're down to, isn't it?"

"It more than *kind of* sucks," she said, with a headshake. "I just can't believe this is what I'm expected to believe is justice."

"It's not justice," Conall agreed, "not in any way. And justice will definitely move slowly in this case because there will be hindrances at every turn."

"Right, but surely Henry would want Jake locked up so he stays safe?"

"That might be an answer for some fathers, but for this one and a lot of others like him? It's likely a big no. I expect Jake to be out on bail in no time."

"Well, damn it," she muttered in frustration. As she got outside, she looked over at his truck and asked, "Are you okay to drive?"

He laughed. "I'm totally okay to drive, though I do need to contact Kat and see if she can give me some advice on that joint, whether it's anything to worry about. The issue would be if it seized up suddenly, and I have no control over that."

"I don't like the sound of that," she replied, looking down at his prosthetic. "You need that leg."

"I sure do," he agreed cheerfully, as he walked over to his

vehicle. "Yet I've been without it before."

She stopped, frowned at him, and asked, "That's why you're also so good to Michael, isn't it? Because you understand what it's like be in a wheelchair."

"I sure do," he admitted. "You don't get to this stage of recovery, not without having been through Michael's stage."

"Could he ever walk again?"

"I don't know," he replied, with a shrug. "I haven't looked into it and don't know anything about his injuries, but I've seen some amazing things happen."

"That would sure make a huge difference to his frame of mind."

"It would certainly make him feel a lot less of a victim, but the reality is that not everybody has enough body part left to put prosthetics on."

"Maybe it's something you can talk to him about."

He chuckled. "I see what's happening here. We are helping Michael now too, aren't we?"

She shrugged and gave him a cheeky grin. "Hey, I'm just picking up on your style. It's not as if you didn't have that going on already."

"Maybe." He smiled. "And we could both do a whole lot worse than reaching out and helping others. It used to be more of a world where everyone helped their neighbors—not like this, where they toss each other to the wolves."

"It seems like that was a long time ago," she muttered, as she stared at him, "but I would really like to think it was possible to go back to something like that."

He nodded. "It doesn't mean that it always has to be so ugly," he pointed out. "The world could very well return to doing better."

"Maybe," she muttered. "Not to change the subject, but

I could use a piece of pie. How about you?"

He frowned at her. "Where do we get pie at this hour? I thought you told me how the town shuts down early."

"It's not that late," she clarified, checking her watch. "Besides, Joe's Diner is open, so we could go there."

"Ah, your mom."

"Yeah, my mom. Absolutely." She shared the directions to get over there.

"We're just having pie?" he asked.

"That's all I want, but suit yourself," she replied. "I just want to see a face I know and love, who knows and loves me," she murmured. "It's been kind of a rough day."

"A rough couple of days actually," he stated, with a nod. "Have you heard anything more from Mel's mother?"

Bethany shook her head. "No, and that's another thing that'll be rough to deal with," she muttered. "Kassie was always really lenient, but Mel's dad was always really strict, so I think we may have another issue here, not like Jake's situation at all, but where Mel has one parent who's got no discipline and the other with so much discipline. Mel couldn't wait to get out of that household."

"From what Michael had said about his sister, I doubt Page got much discipline either. Yet I don't think either case warrants the reactions that both Mel and Page have had."

"I agree," Bethany added, "though it does make me a little worried about having kids."

He nodded. "I'm with you there, not that it's likely to ever happen in my case."

"Why not?" she asked. "Don't you want any, or can't you have any?" She glanced down at the leg as she spoke, wondering if she had gone too far.

"As far as I know, I can. I just don't have a partner willing to have a family with me—or any partner at the moment," he shared, with a smile.

"Right. … Neither do I," she muttered, a little abashed. "It's been a long time since I even had a decent relationship."

"Ditto, and, when someone is broken and busted up, like Michael and me, it makes relationships particularly hard to start and even harder to explain, when questions about the injuries arise."

"Are there more injuries than what I can see?" she asked, twisting in the front seat to look at him, "because you don't look terribly damaged to me. Oh, God, I'm so sorry. That sounded so trite and insensitive. I should just shut up."

"You're fine. I am actually happy to see that you are willing to have a candid conversation about it. So, aside from the physical damage, there'll always be a certain level of psychological damage," he shared. "Sometimes I wake up in the middle of the night. The PTSD takes hold, and my nightmares? Well, they can get a little scary. However, for the most part, therapy and rehab has taken care of the worst of it."

"I would say it's taken care of way more than the worst of it," she replied. "You look beyond well-adjusted."

He laughed. "And that is a complete fib."

She grinned. "Okay, fine. So I exaggerated a bit."

He smiled at her. "That's just because you want to see all the good things in people."

"Sure. I do want to see the good in people and the good happening for them. I've seen so much of the crappy side of life that I really want to believe the good stuff is out there."

"And there is," he stated, with that same smile.

"Absolutely there is." She pointed up ahead as they approached the edge of the town limits. "Around the next block is the cafe."

He followed her directions and pulled up outside. "Do you want to text them and let them know it's us?"

"No need. They're still open."

As they went in, Bethany looked around and found nobody here. She frowned and called out, "Mom, are you here?" When no answer came, Bethany called out, "Joe?"

When still no answer came, she looked over at Conall in alarm, and they both raced through the main part of the restaurant, which was completely empty, and into the back, where the kitchen was. They found her mom, sitting on the floor, sobbing, as she cradled Joe's head. She looked up as they arrived and started to sob harder.

Bethany cried out, "I'm calling 9-1-1."

Conall nodded. "What happened?" Conall asked, as he crouched beside Rosalind, checking Joe for a pulse, "He's still alive."

"No, no, he's gone," Rosalind replied, bawling hard. Bethany now sat on the floor, next to her mom, holding her.

"No, he's not," Conall clarified. "Let's lay him flat, so he can breathe. … Easy now. I can feel a pulse." Rosalind stared at him in shock, as if finally hearing Conall. "He's lost an awful lot of blood." He looked to Bethany. "See if you can get the story out of her."

But Bethany had already called for an ambulance, so her mom bolted to her feet and raced outside. Bethany raced after her. "Mom, what's going on? Where are you going?"

"After them," she roared.

"After who?"

"Those stupid kids."

"Hang on a minute. Are we talking about the same punks as before? Jake and his cronies?"

"No, no, not them, the others. She works for you, … the one you used to babysit," Rosalind cried out. "How could she do this to us?"

"Wait. Are you talking about Melanie?"

Her mother turned and looked at her. "Yes, that stupid smart-mouthed girl. She was here with some guy, who I don't even know."

"Ah, crap, … and she shot Joe?"

"No, *he* shot Joe. Good-for-nothing kids. Joe wouldn't give him free food and declared he didn't need more freeloaders around here. And they just shot him. He just up and shot him. It caught him low in the gut, and he went down like a huge log," she cried out. "I mean, he's a big man. I couldn't believe it."

"How long ago was this?" Bethany asked.

"Just a few minutes," her mom whispered. "I thought he was dead. He didn't answer me, and it didn't seem like he was breathing."

"He's not dead, and, if anybody can help him, Conall can," she said, taking her mother in her arms. "Did you see where they went?"

"No, they just bolted out back. That kid mentioned something about you, but I didn't understand it."

"Can you tell me exactly what he said?"

"No, not exactly, it all happened so fast, you know? It was just a slam, something about mother and daughter, both bitches."

"Of course," she muttered. "It seems he's unraveling very quickly."

"Is that what you call it?" she asked, sobbing harder. "What has happened to this town? It used to be such a lovely place to live, and now we just want to sell this place and go."

"That might not be a bad idea," Bethany agreed, then realized she should make another call. She quickly dialed the number that Greg had given her. When he answered, he sounded busy.

"We're still not done here."

"You may not be done there, but the other nightmare in our world, the young couple, … Melanie and Michael's nephew, Page, … they have shot my mother's partner over here at the restaurant. We've called for an ambulance, but I'm not certain Joe will make it." At that, her mother sobbed anew. "He's been gut shot, and he's down. He's a big man, and he's lost a lot of blood. Conall is doing what he can."

"We're on the way," Greg stated. "Do you know what happened to the shooter?"

"They took off out the back. Just a second." She turned to look at her mother. "Mom, listen to me. Did they have a vehicle?"

Rosalind nodded. "Yes, they did. I heard it noisily tear off, but I don't know what it was. I didn't see it. I was on the floor with Joe."

"They initially stole Michael's vehicle. Oh, wait. Did they take Joe's truck? I didn't see his truck in the lot."

Her mom stared at Bethany. "I don't know," her mom whispered, "maybe."

Bethany spoke to Greg on the other line now, hearing him in a moving vehicle now. "I'm checking to see if Joe's truck is here. That may be the one they've stolen." She raced around the corner. "I can't see it anywhere, so it's very possible that's what they're in." She quickly gave him the make, model, and color details. "I don't know the license plate," she shared, then turned back to look at her mother, who shook her head. "Yeah, you'll have to look it up. My mom doesn't know it either, but she's pretty rattled."

"It's okay. We can get it," Greg replied. "Any reason your mom didn't call the sheriff's office?"

"Yeah, nobody here believes in the authorities anymore. Plus my mother was in shock and thought Joe was dead, but Conall found a pulse. Mom might have called 9-1-1 if anybody else had been here. I did call for an ambulance and assumed that *should* get the deputies rolling as well, but I doubt it right now. I guess you can decide."

"Conall?" Greg asked.

"He's inside with Joe. I can tell you that Conall's itching to get Joe headed to a hospital. Then Conall wants to go on a hunt."

"Of course he does." Greg sighed. "See if you can cage him a little bit."

She could hardly control herself. "I would like to let loose the animal inside him," she snapped. "We've taken so much shit, and this won't end well. I'm damn tired of looking after other people's kids and trying to keep them from screwing up their whole lives, but, at the rate Page and Mel are going, along with that bully Jake, they may not survive the week."

"I know. Try to stay calm though," Greg added. "I hear you. I'm just glad your mom didn't get shot."

"Oh my God, I didn't even ask if she was hurt. Shit, just get here fast, will you?" She hung up and turned to look at her mother. "Are you hurt at all? Did he shoot you?"

Her mom frowned, then shook her head. "No, no, he didn't shoot me. ... That damn kid just laughed when he shot Joe."

"Of course he did." Bethany groaned. "There's just no end to the punk-ass pieces of shit in this world, is there?"

"I don't know what Joe ever did to him," she whispered, "but the damn kid wanted free food. He told us how he had heard from a friend that you could get all kinds of free food here, and he was hungry. And Joe? … That was the last straw, and he just lost it."

"I can totally understand that."

"Joe was like, *Hell no, we've had enough of punks like you coming in here looking for free food, so forget it.* Honestly I told him how we should just give it to them, but Joe didn't listen." She started to sob all over again. "We're not making ends meet here, and we can't keep giving everything away."

"Of course not, and you shouldn't have to. Better to close the doors than have these kids treat you like that."

Her mom sobbed harder and nodded. "That's what I told Joe, but he wanted to sell the business first. That way we could leave and get a start somewhere else. Yet how do we sell a business that's failing because of these punks?" she asked. "We couldn't put that on anybody else."

She winced for her mother's sake, as Bethany thought about everything they'd been through. "I'm so sorry," she whispered.

"It's not your fault, honey. I'm just sorry that we stayed in this town. We should have gotten out of here a long time ago."

"Maybe we still can," she muttered.

"What about you? You've already invested so much in your business. Your clinic is doing so well …"

"It has, but if I need to shut it down and move somewhere else? … Well, that'll be a huge expense, but if it needs to happen, it needs to happen," she whispered. "Besides, this can't keep happening. I don't want to turn around one day and find out you've been shot, just trying to defend your restaurant."

"Yet that's exactly what happened tonight," she stated, as she turned back toward the building. "I need to go see Joe," she muttered, getting frantic again.

Immediately Bethany led her mom back inside. As soon as she took one look at Conall, she knew it was bad. "The ambulance is on the way, and so is Greg."

He nodded. "Good, I need some assistance."

Bethany studied Joe, frowned, then spoke to her mom. "I need something to make a tourniquet out of, Mom. Joe's got way-too-much bleeding, and he took a second bullet in the leg."

"I didn't realize that." Conall gave her a shake of his head.

"His leg too?" her mom asked, frozen in place.

"Holy shit," Bethany muttered. "Yeah, Mom, get me, … I don't care, a strap, a belt, a tie, something. I've got to slow the bleeding."

Her mom raced to the far side of the kitchen and came back with some zap straps.

"Okay, good." Conall quickly made a tourniquet, and almost immediately the blood underneath Joe's leg started to slow down.

Then Bethany jumped into action. "It's okay, Mom. I need you to sit down." Bethany did a full check on Joe, as Conall watched her.

"I should have had you do that to begin with," Conall admitted. "You would have caught it earlier."

"Doesn't matter. I was distracted too." She waved a hand about. "I should have done a lot of things differently today. I haven't been acting my best," she shared, with a headshake. "It's been a very long day, and my brain's not clear, but it's clearing up quickly now."

"Good, that will help, and hopefully we'll get through this."

She smiled at him through a sheen of tears. "I hope so. I don't know what the hell I would have done with all this shit if you hadn't been here to help me."

"You're doing just fine," he replied.

She checked Joe over again. "We need to keep him breathing and be prepared to jump into CPR, if his heart stops. Yet he's a tough one." In the distance, she heard the ambulance, and, with a wave of relief, she announced, "I'll bring them back here."

She raced outside as they pulled in, and, within seconds, she had them working on Joe. Ten minutes later, Joe was hooked up to oxygen, various monitors, and an IV. He was rolled out of the restaurant on the gurney and into the back of the ambulance.

Her mom already sat there in the jump seat, waiting. Bethany looked over at her. "I'll meet you at the hospital soon."

Her mother nodded, barely acknowledging her, as she focused her attention on Joe.

"They're really an item, aren't they?" Conall asked.

"They have been for years," Bethany said, her tears spilling over now. "She's a good person, but a lot of people look down on her." She shook her head. "Small towns can be hard, and a lot of people don't appreciate the fact that she's with a black man."

"I know that you are committed to your business here, but is there any chance you want to relocate?"

"I was just talking to Mom about that very thing. I don't want her staying here, not if this is the kind of treatment she's constantly dealing with."

"No, of course not," he muttered. He pulled her up close and kissed her on the temple. "I'm sorry."

"Me too," she murmured, as she wrapped her arms around him. She tilted her head up to face him and smiled. "Have I told you yet how much I appreciate the fact that you came to town to find Bacchus?"

CONALL CHUCKLED. "NO, not in so many words, … but it's definitely been a little more difficult here than just finding a lost War Dog. I'll give you that."

"It sure has been," she muttered. "Yeah, it's been quite the ride. I need some sleep, but I've got to head down to the hospital to be with my mom."

He nodded. "Let's go grab some food, and we'll take it to the hospital."

She looked around the café and frowned. "I better clean up this mess first. I don't want her coming back to this."

"No, you can't," he told her, reaching out a hand to stop her. "The authorities need to gather forensics evidence first."

She groaned. "I should have known that. Sorry. I'll just have to come back and do it later."

"We'll both come back," he stated. "It's not terrible, but someone will come in here and take a look for the record."

"Do you really think anybody will?"

"Yes," he stated. "If nothing else, Greg will get photos and look for any evidence, and he'll definitely bring a team down."

"Fine," she muttered. "I'm too tired to argue."

"Let's go get some food," he suggested. "We can't get it

here because the deputies will be here soon."

She smiled. I've done my fair share of cooking in this kitchen," she muttered, as she stared around at it, "but maybe it is time they made a change."

"Chances are it's time," he declared firmly, "but first things first. Let's get you some fuel, before you run out of gas and drop."

"I know. I know."

Just then came a yell from Greg out front. He walked into the back and shared, "Just passed the ambulance on the way."

She nodded grimly. "Joe's in pretty rough shape. We found a second gunshot wound in his leg."

He shook his head. "And your mom was sure who it was?"

Bethany nodded. "Yes, it was my ex-employee, Melanie, and her boyfriend, Page, who is Michael's nephew."

"Jeez," Greg muttered, "you would think they wouldn't be so stupid as that."

"We better warn Michael that they're still in town," Conall said suddenly.

She stared at him and winced. "Yes, that definitely needs to happen too, but I also need to get to the hospital."

Conall looked over at Greg. "I'll leave this to you. Did you bring the locals along?"

"I did," he replied, with a nod. "A couple of them are on the way, and we'll handle this." Looking at Bethany, he repeated, "And *we* will handle it. I promise. Then I'll get over to the hospital as soon as I can."

She nodded. "You handle this. I'm heading to the hospital now." She looked over at Conall. "And you need to go check on Michael."

"Got it," he agreed. "Let's go. I'll take you to the hospital first and will come by later, and we'll grab your wheels, so that you're not stuck here." He eyed her intently, still seeing some shock on her face. "Your car's still at your apartment because we came together in my truck to the sheriff's office."

"*Right*. I can't think straight yet. Plus I'm supposed to be at the clinic tomorrow," she muttered, "but I'm exhausted, and my mom needs me too."

"Can't you close the clinic and maybe reschedule those appointments?" Conall suggested.

"Yeah, some of it anyway," she muttered, "but first I need to check on Mom and Joe."

They waved to Greg, and after arriving at the hospital, Conall let Bethany out. Then he headed over to see Michael.

He drove into the driveway and then stopped because he saw shadows through curtain to the living room window, and somebody was inside, but it wasn't Danny or his mother. Her car was gone.

Opening the door to his truck, he hopped out, still wondering about damage to his leg but not having the time to do a thorough check. Walking up to the front door, he wished he was armed, since he still couldn't see who was inside. When he rang the doorbell, he got no answer, though it was also pretty late.

He called out. "Michael, it's me." But again he got no answer. There had been a light on inside and an obvious shadow seen, which meant somebody was home just one minute ago. That didn't mean it was the right somebody though. He pushed open the door and stepped inside, coming face-to-face with a very pissed-off Page, pointing a gun at him, which by Conall's count was the third time today. And three times was too many, as far as he was concerned.

# CHAPTER 14

E NTERING THE HOSPITAL hallway, Bethany mustered her strength and put a smile on her face, all the while gearing up for what was ahead. She walked down the hallway to where her mother sat on a bench. Looking up, her mom raced over, and the two women fell into each other's arms.

"He's alive," her mom said, "but that's all I can tell you. He's in surgery right now."

"That was fast."

Mom nodded. "They had to get control of the bleeding." She held her daughter tight, and the two just stood there together.

"He'll be okay," Bethany replied. "I believe that."

Her mother tilted her head back to see her face and smiled. "I do too." Yet still so heartbroken, her eyes swollen, her mom added, "It's definitely time for a change."

"Oh, I agree, and it's a good time to be thinking about it too."

The two women sat down on the bench, as they discussed options. Old Joe would need some help after this.

"We've never lived together, though it's always been a bone of contention between us."

"*That's* just become a nonissue." Bethany chuckled. "Let's just say it's a really good time to take advantage of it."

Her mom smiled. "We've been spending most nights

together anyway," she muttered, "but he's just stubborn. He never wanted to damage my reputation—any more than it already is."

At that, Bethany shook her head. "Maybe we should find a place to live where he would be comfortable and where an interracial relationship would not raise eyebrows. This place has always been pretty tough for that."

"I know. I just couldn't leave because you were here."

"What? I didn't leave because you were here," Bethany shared.

Her mom stared at her, then finally smiled. "That sounds like a good idea. So, maybe we all need to leave together," she suggested hopefully. "But what about your business?"

"I know. I'll have to close up the clinic, and I'll start fresh again," she muttered, "and that isn't something I'm looking forward to, but I don't really see that there's much of a future here."

"I think you're right. The town itself is struggling."

"Is that the word for it?" Bethany asked, with a small smile. "I think it's way more than *struggling*, but it is what it is."

They were still talking about options and locations, when the doctor came over to see them. Mom bounced to her feet, fear all over her face, as her question came out as a whisper, "How is he, Doctor?"

"He came through the surgery just fine. We got the bullets out. He should make a full recovery, but it'll take some time," he pointed out. "He won't be allowed to work for a while, and he'll have to stay in the hospital for several days, if not more," he muttered, "depending on how it goes. Whether and how he handles it or fights it is key. We can't have him ripping out any stitches, and that abdomen wound is touch-and-go as it is. I would say at least a week here at a minimum, so we can sedate him and keep him as immobile as possible."

Her mother just nodded, but tears were in her eyes, as she clasped the doctor's hand and whispered, "Thank you, for everything."

He smiled at her and nodded. "Everybody needs to be loved, especially when healing. So you can stay here and wait a little bit, if you want. We'll bring him out of recovery soon, and, when we get him settled into his room, you can spend some time with him there."

"Can I stay with him?" she asked anxiously. "I mean, overnight and every day."

He hesitated and then shrugged. "Why not," he murmured. "I think it will probably do you both some good."

Bethany smiled at the doctor, as he walked away, because the doctor was right. It did everybody good when you were surrounded by loved ones. She looked over at her mom. "Why don't I get you over to your house, and you can pick up some clothes for your stay, at least for overnight?"

Her mom just shook her head. "I don't want to leave him."

"Okay, I'll just catch a cab to get my car, then go to your place and grab you an overnight bag. How's that?"

She looked at her gratefully. "That would be awesome."

"Okay, that's the plan."

"Are you sure you don't want to wait for Conall?" her mom asked, looking over at her.

"I think he'll probably meet me at my house anyway," she muttered. "He's gone to talk to Michael. Then we were planning on spending the night at my place."

Her mother grinned. "Is it serious?"

At that, Bethany flushed. "I don't even know what the hell it is," she muttered. "Aside from it being just a safety viewpoint amid all this trouble, I hardly even know the man."

"Yes, you do," Mom replied, with a surety in her voice that Bethany had always respected. "You know exactly what it is. You just weren't expecting it today."

"I wasn't expecting it at all," Bethany declared, glancing at her mom. "That's how it was for you and Dad though, wasn't it?"

"It absolutely was," Mom stated, with a bright smile. "The best years of my life. These past few years, they've been tough, just because of the bullies and this town's viewpoint of our relationship," she noted, "but I've got no complaints about Joe. I didn't expect to care about someone again as much as I do. Joe is, … well, he's pretty special in his own way."

"I've known that for quite some time, Mom," Bethany confirmed. "There's no reason the two of you can't live long and happy lives together," she muttered. "We just need to get through this part."

With that said, Bethany headed outside and hailed a cab, texting Conall as she headed home. She just needed to get her wheels and then she could go over to her mother's house, pack her a bag, and get it back to the hospital. As long as her mother was happy and content at Joe's side, that's where she should stay.

In the meantime, they had to shut down Joe's Diner, including posting signs saying it was closed, possibly forever. That fact didn't cause her any pain either.

She had a longstanding love/hate relationship with the

diner, and, for that matter, she had a love/hate relationship with the town. They hadn't been very accepting of Joe, even though he'd been here for a very long time, but it had to weigh on a man getting those racist looks and dark comments. It was definitely time to get them to a place where they could live a happier and peaceful life.

There had been no response from Conall, when the cab dropped her off at her apartment building. She headed inside, raced up the stairs to her second-floor apartment. She quickly changed her clothes because she hadn't had a chance since dealing with Joe. Then she got out one of her carry-on bags. As she went to grab her purse, she realized it had been moved.

She froze, and then she heard the voice behind her. "Did you really think you'd get off so easily?"

She turned around to see Jake standing there, not with the same gun but another gun, bigger, heavier, much more awkward looking and twice as powerful. She shook her head at him. "I don't have time for this right now," she snapped. "My mom is at the hospital. Joe's been shot, probably by one of your daddy's guns," she snapped, "and right now I just can't deal with you."

"What do you mean he's been shot?" Jake asked, completely sidelined by her question.

"The other punk in town, Page, is still here, and you probably sold him the gun too."

Jake frowned and then shrugged. "I did sell someone a gun recently. He wanted to pull off a couple heists to grab some money, so he can get out of town."

"Yeah, that would be him, and now he's shot my mother's partner, so the café is effectively closed. You and your gang can forget about getting any more freebies from there."

He stiffened at that. "I don't like their damn coffee anyway. It tastes like sludge."

"*Yeah*, and yet you went there every day," she noted, with a headshake. She pointed at the weapon. "So, now you've got another one of Daddy's weapons, and he'll be held responsible for this, after leaving shit available for you to grab."

"You don't know anything about it," he snapped. "Dear old Dad seems to be having a change of heart, and that is something I blame you for."

She snorted. "Your dad should have had a change of heart a long time ago. You're a piece of shit, and you're going to jail, and you know it." She knew she was treading on troubled waters, but she didn't care. She'd reached her limit today and just couldn't be bullied anymore. Even though she might take a bullet for it, she really didn't have time for his nonsense.

She waved him off. "I've got to pack a bag for my mom and get it to the hospital. Then I have to check up on Michael. Plus I also have clinic hours tomorrow." She looked around for her purse. Seeing it on the couch, she snagged it, ignoring him. "So, I don't know what the hell you think you're doing here," she snapped, "but I don't have time for it."

Just as she went to open the door, a bullet hit the wall right beside her. She closed her eyes, then turned to glare at him. "You don't want to do this with me, especially not now."

"Oh, but I do want to do this." Jake smiled. "Because, if nothing else, I know it'll hurt that cripple you hang around with. I mean, ... what a pair. Your mom's with that big black asshole, and here you are, with a cripple. Like, what the hell's up with that?"

She faced him. "Both of them are twice the man you'll ever be." She glared at him. "Why else do you need that gun?"

He stared at her. "Why the hell aren't you afraid?"

"Because I'm tired of being afraid," she declared. "I'm tired of letting insecure people like you walk all over me. I'm tired of listening to my poor mother talk about how you keep chasing their customers away with your bullying ways, stealing from them by not paying for what you consume, and being a constant threat just lurking around in her life. You don't understand what it's like to live with worry and fear all the time, and you just don't give a damn." She shook her head. "Guys like you should have just been put away when you were born, so the world didn't have to deal with you. Or maybe just exterminated."

He stared at her in shock. "You can't talk to me like that," he replied in a blustering tone.

"I just did," she snapped, "so what will you do about it?"

He hesitated, as if he was completely unsure of what to do.

She nodded. "You're confused because you don't understand the basic functioning of normal human relationships."

"Shut—"

"Why? Is the truth not sitting right with you? You think it's all fun and games and that you just get to be this all-powerful bully? That's not how life works," she stated, with a shake of her head. "You really ought to be pitied. I just don't have any more pity left for you."

"I don't need your pity," he shouted, the gun immediately coming back up again.

"Yeah, that's good because nobody'll pity you when you

get to trial. Nobody'll pity you when you're in court and when they listen to all the tales from everybody in town about how you bullied them and how you cheated them and how you stole from them and how you threatened them, day after day after day."

"No one will say anything."

"That remains to be seen. No pity left for a piece of shit like you," she repeated and headed out. "I don't know what the hell you think you'll pull right now, so you just need to shoot me dead and officially become a murderer, meaning your life will be 100 percent over. Even if the dysfunctional local justice system doesn't put you away, you can bet that, one way or another, … Conall will."

He paled at that thought, and she nodded. In a surprise move, she pulled back her purse and ran right at him. Almost immediately his hands went up over his head, as he tried to protect himself. "Stop it. Stop it! You're a bloody crazy woman."

"I'm not a crazy woman," she argued through gritted teeth, striking him over the head with her purse again and again. "I'm a woman who is fed up. I've reached the end of my rope, and trust me. I'm not going down easy."

And, with that, she kept hitting him, prepared to tear him apart with her bare hands.

He took one final look at that expression on her face and bolted out the door.

Now that Jake was gone, she stood in her living room and started to laugh, a panicked, hysterical laughter that only stopped when the tears started to pour. She slowly sagged in place, only to remember that she had a mother to take care of, and Conall was still potentially coming.

Drying her eyes and telling herself that she needed a long

holiday when this shit was over, she got into her car. Glad to have her own vehicle back, she then phoned Greg and told him what happened. "I'm now on my way to my mother's place to pack her a bag for the hospital," she added, "but Jake will probably run home to his daddy right now."

"You beat him up with your purse?" Greg asked, with a note of amusement very obvious, even over the phone.

"Yeah, and you don't need to tell me how stupid it was. I'm sure Conall will rip into me something good, when he finds out."

"And so he should," Greg agreed, with a chuckle. "On the other hand, … I really hope you have some of that on tape."

She froze, and then she snorted. "I never stop the cameras, so it would have been recording. So, yeah, it's got to be there on my system."

"Is your apartment locked?" he asked briskly.

"Sure, not that locks do very much good, it seems," she muttered. "As it is, I've got nothing to worry about saving and nothing to protect in the first place. Why?"

"Because I want to retrieve it."

"It's accessible from my phone, so when I get to my mom's place, I'll send it to you, okay?"

"Good job. By the way, have you talked to Conall?"

She pulled up in front of her mother's place. Bethany got out, still speaking to Greg. "No, I haven't yet, but he went over to Michael's to warn him about the nephew."

"*Right.* I've texted him a couple times, but I haven't heard back."

She quickly flipped through her phone, brought up her security cameras, and started to laugh when she saw the most recent footage. "Oh my God, no wonder he ran. I look like a crazy woman."

"You were, I'm sure. Somebody who's hit the end of her rope. Don't feel bad about it. Just send me the video, and I'll get him picked up."

"Do you really think they'll charge him for it?"

"He broke into your apartment again, brandishing another weapon, threatening you with said weapon, all after being released on bail, *with* a promise not to have anything to do with you," he stated, his tone deepening with disgust. "So, yeah, this time, he's not getting out."

"And you might want to see if the gun Page used to shoot Joe was bought off of Jake. He mentioned a gun sale to me. Anyway I just emailed the tape to you," she said, then stopped. "What was that about Conall?"

"I haven't heard from him, after texting him a couple times."

"Oh God," she muttered, "I haven't heard back from him either. You need to get over there right away."

He stopped and asked, "Seriously?"

"Yeah, seriously," she muttered. "The only way he wouldn't have contacted one of us was if that asshole Page is there."

"I'm already on my way," Greg confirmed. "You get to the hospital and look after your mom. We've got this." And, with that, he hung up.

She thought about it and shook her head. Conall had been there for her every step of the way. She wouldn't let him down now.

She raced to her mom's small apartment, packed a bag for just tonight. "I can always come back tomorrow and get more stuff for her, but I need to get over to Michael's place," she murmured.

She sped all the way to the hospital, dropped off the bag with her mom—sitting beside Joe, who appeared unconscious, but Bethany assumed he was still sedated. She leaned over, kissed her mother, and whispered, "I've got to go." She returned to her vehicle and raced outside, heading toward Michael's place, grateful the hospital was on the outskirts of the town over making it a slightly shorter drive.

When she pulled up, she was hoping Greg would already be here, but she didn't see his vehicle. She had no idea what to expect or what she was supposed to do. Yet she stepped up to the front door and walked in without any notice. Conall sat on the couch, pain evident on his face, and the same girl who Bethany used to babysit sat beside him, tears in her eyes, as she stared up at her boyfriend.

"We can't just kill everybody," she cried out.

"We have to," Page stated brutally, "because they're all going to rat us out."

Michael and Greg were here too, all seated before gun-toting Page.

"Wow," Bethany announced, as she stood here, her hands on her hips. "What is this? A bloody tea party and you forgot to invite me?" She looked over at Mel. "You didn't turn out so well." she snapped, still pissed from her outing with Jake.

Mel burst into tears. Getting up, she ran over and wrapped her arms around Bethany, sobbing. Caught off guard and unsure of what else to do, Bethany held the immature young woman as she cried.

"I don't know what's going on, Bethany. We were never supposed to kill this many."

"But you were okay to kill *some*?" she asked, pulling back and looking at her. "You're okay to pick and choose who to kill?"

At that, Page snorted. "I know, right? I just told her that. *You can't just pick and choose.* When we're in this, we're in it."

"But I didn't mean for it to go this far," Mel cried out.

"I guess you should have taken a second to think about it." Bethany stared at her, realizing she had never really understood who this young woman really was. "How many people have you shot so far? Never mind. I don't want to hear it. What I do want to know is that this is finished."

"Of course it's done," Mel wailed, as she turned to look at Page. "Right? It's over, and we're not doing this anymore."

He laughed at her. "Sorry, sweetheart. In for a penny, in for a pound."

"And yet you know your uncle doesn't have any money, since you already took it all," Bethany stated.

"He had more coming, but somebody went and stopped his pension from being dropped into his account."

Bethany looked at him. "Are you telling me that the little bit of pension he gets every month is enough to make a difference in your life? I don't think so. It's not enough for Michael now, and taking that little bit of money won't get you anywhere."

"Oh, it'll get me somewhere," he argued, "but the account was changed."

"Did you think he wouldn't try and keep the only income source that he has?" she asked, staring at him in surprise. "Are you really that stupid?"

"Don't call me stupid," Page yelled.

"What will your mom think about all this?" Michael asked. Bacchus sat at his side, his head resting on Michael's lap but his gaze intent on Page. And Bacchus's muscles pumped, as if ready for anything.

Bethany looked over at Michael. "I'm so sorry, Michael, that you had to endure betrayal from a blood relative."

Michael nodded. "It's my fault. I shouldn't have taken him in. You never really know who people are until it blows up in your face."

"I do know, and I'm sorry you had to find out," she whispered. "It happened to me as well, with *this* one." She still held Mel close, with an arm around her, even as Bethany tried to figure out what was going on, but she knew this was a dangerous flash point. She looked over at Conall and Greg, then asked, "Are you two okay?"

"Of course they're okay," Page replied in irritation. "I mean, no point in killing anybody I need, is there?"

"I don't know," Bethany countered. "Seems to me that you and Jake are a great fit."

"No way, he's an idiot," Page replied, with a dismissive glance.

"And yet that's where you got the gun, isn't it?"

He shrugged. "Yes. So what if we got the gun from him? That doesn't make a difference, does it?"

"Just another nail in Jake's coffin and yours, now that it's been used in a violent crime spree. That won't go well for him or you."

Page snorted. "That's what's wrong with the world. People have all these rules, but they don't apply to me—or to him." He waved the gun around, as if to make his point.

Bethany laughed. "You might have another think about that, while sitting in prison," she added, with a smirk. "Jake's not having a very good day as it is, so you might want to avoid a run-in with him."

Page frowned at her. "I don't give a shit about that

punk. I just want to get the hell out of here."

"Oh, I get it. I hear you," she said, with a nod. "Absolutely. I mean it's all about you, right?"

"Yeah, it *is* all about me," he declared, waving the gun in her face. "And you? … You just need to shut the fuck up. I'm tired of this chattering." He turned to his uncle and bellowed, "I'll start killing people, unless you tell me where the money is."

Bacchus rose, as the gun turned in his direction. "The money or the dog is first."

"YOU HAVE THE money, idiot," Conall stated, taking a step closer to the dog.

Page stared at him in frustration. "You go to his laptop. You're the one who set this all up, aren't you?"

Conall nodded, then walked over to the laptop.

"Now you transfer that money into my account, right now," Page ordered, "or I'll start popping people."

Conall looked over at Michael, and he nodded, then said, "I guess I can get by on food stamps for another month."

"Yeah, and what will you do when he comes back in a month because he needs more money?" Conall asked.

"No way. I'll take all the accounts with me," Page announced. "I'm not letting you change all that shit again."

His uncle just stared at him. "You lazy piece of shit. All you have to do is get a job."

"I'm not getting a job, am I?" He glared at him. "And I don't intend to ever. You can work and even when you can't do anything, they still pay you, so I might as well just keep getting the money from you."

"You know that can't continue, right?" Conall asked. "Life isn't quite so simple. You know that, right?"

"I'm not stupid."

Conall made a sound in the back of his throat. "You're sure acting like it."

At that, when the gun whipped back and came down hard against his head, he tilted to the side and let the force of the jolt take him backward, but he also had a hand on Page's gun arm, bringing it down as Conall fell. Bacchus leapt forward and latched onto Page's gunhand and dragged him to the ground. The gun fired into the floor, as Mel screamed in terror, but Conall already had him pinned in place, as Greg picked up the gun and held it on him.

"So now what?" Greg yelled at Page, over all the ruckus. Bacchus's deep gut-wrenching howls in the back of his throat were never at full volume, as he was too busy grinding his teeth on Page's arm. Meanwhile, screams were coming from Page …

Conall immediately calmed Bacchus down, finally getting him to release Page and to stand guard. Michael wheeled over and placed a hand on Bacchus, who immediately sat back, more relaxed now that he'd done his part.

"You'll have quite a few years to sit in jail and to think about your actions." Greg shook his head. "What a waste."

"I'm going to kill that fucking dog," Page yelled in obvious pain. "No way in hell I'll be in jail. And now, with this dog attack, I won't have to. They will let me off, after that piece of shit hurt me."

"Nope, they won't. He was defending his owner against an armed attacker." Conall eyed him in amusement for a moment, then asked, "So what's your plan B?"

Looking over at Mel, Page said, "You know what to do."

"I can't," she whimpered.

"We agreed," he yelled. "Do it."

She started to quiver and shake. "No, I can't."

"What are you supposed to do?" Bethany asked her, keeping a firm grip on the girl.

Melanie slowly pulled a very tiny handgun from her pocket. "I'm supposed to shoot him and then myself."

"That's not happening," Bethany snapped, and, tugging it out of Mel's hand, she looked over at Page. "And just like that, … plan B is off the table."

He started swearing and fighting, kicking and twisting hard against Conall's grip, but Conall wasn't having any of it. With Michael barely managing to keep Bacchus from jumping back into the fray, Conall held down Page, and very quickly Greg was there with ties to secure the struggling man.

He could fight all he wanted now, but he was just thumping his head and limbs against the hard floor. Finally he stopped screaming and just laid there for a time. In a tone so cold with promise, he muttered, "I'll get you."

"Keep talking," Conall urged. "I'll make sure the judge hears every word." He had his phone recording and held it out for Page to see the steady red light.

Page screamed again, loud and obnoxiously, in a fit of pure temper. As soon as he ran dry again, Conall smiled and added, "It will make for a really good hearing, when we get to the court case."

"Yeah, it sure will," Greg agreed, with a nod.

"How many years do you think he'll get?" Conall asked Greg.

"Fifteen to life at least, and so will she," Greg replied,

turning a hard gaze over at Mel.

She started bawling immediately. "I didn't do anything," she cried out.

"Yes, you did," Bethany said.

"But I just stole little bit of money from you," she admitted, tears streaming down her face. "Surely that fifty bucks isn't a big deal."

"It was more than fifty bucks, and you know it. Still, it wasn't as big a deal as compared to shooting people. For every shot Page fired, you will pay the same price," Bethany stated, staring at her. "For Page shooting Old Joe, you'll be charged as an accessory, with my mom as a witness."

"No, but—"

"It's all fun and games, until you get caught," Bethany stated, "and now you have to face the consequences, just like everybody else in this town has."

Mel dropped to the floor, sobbing hysterically.

Bethany looked over at Conall. "Should we check her for other weapons?"

He rolled his eyes, then stepped up and did a quick frisk of the screaming girl on the floor, who was even now fighting him.

"Leave me alone! Don't touch me! Get away from me!" she screamed at him, "I hate you. I hate you all!"

"Not half as much as you'll hate your life coming up," Greg shared, as he stared at her. "You have no idea."

She went back to sobbing on the floor, completely incoherent.

Conall walked over and wrapped Bethany in his arms. "Are you okay?"

She nodded. "Yeah. Did Greg tell you what happened to me earlier?"

"No. Is it Joe? Don't tell me—"

Greg interrupted him. "She's had a hell of any evening already." Looking over at the two of them, Greg gave her a wry grin. "Instead of telling you about it, I'll show you." He pulled up the video that she'd sent him and let it play for everybody.

"Oh my God," Bethany muttered, staring at it for the second time this evening, "That's just too much. I look like an idiot."

Michael smiled at her in delight. "Oh my gosh, I love it. You look like that crazy lady from the viral video." He looked over and asked, in between bouts of laughter, "Any chance I can get a copy, for those days when I'm down and think life isn't worth living?" Then he broke off into peals of laughter.

"Okay, very funny, Michael."

"Sure, it is. It's gold. Something like this is worth everything."

She rolled her eyes at him. "Honestly I just want to go away for a very long holiday."

"Yeah?" Conall asked, looking over at her. "Any destination in mind?"

Her gaze twinkled as she asked, "Have *you* got any destination in mind?"

He nodded. "I'm thinking an isolated cabin up in the Colorado Rockies or maybe a beach a very long way from here."

"Either one would work perfectly for me," she said, "but I have to ensure Mom and Joe are doing okay first."

"I think they'll be just fine," Conall suggested. "Now the larger question is where will you end up at the end of the day?"

"I don't know," she admitted, "but I do know that a major rethink needs to happen."

He shook his head. "You've already done the thinking. All you have to do is settle on a new location, and it may not be all that hard."

"Maybe not," she agreed, "but it's got to be someplace where Joe is welcome."

He nodded. "Of course. We won't have it any other way."

She looked at him suspiciously. "I suppose you'll say New Mexico?"

He chuckled. "It could be New Mexico, but it could be somewhere else too. I'm totally okay to move. Yet I do own the family homestead down there, and I would like to keep it."

She smiled. "Maybe we should have another talk about that."

Sirens began to fill the air. As he went to answer the door, she looked at the others. "As long as we can find a place that makes us all happy, I'm game. I do need to go to the clinic tomorrow and for the next few days, but I think I'll be shutting it down pretty soon after that."

"Sounds good to me," Conall muttered. "Let's get this wrapped up, then go crash and just focus on getting through the next few days."

And that's what they did.

# CHAPTER 15

AFTER ALMOST A week of working at the clinic together, Bethany locked the front door, then walked to Conall and said, "Hey, … I guess that's it."

He looked up, smiled, and nodded. "Good enough." He checked his watch. "We're right on schedule. The plane leaves for Hawaii in about six hours."

As she looked around, sadness filled her eyes.

"We can come back to visit, you know?" he muttered.

"I know, but it's definitely time to be moving on. The town is dying, people are moving away, and I can't find a qualified receptionist, so we need to go somewhere else."

"What about your other staff?"

"I just have Liza and Adam, and he's already looking for a new part-time job," she noted.

Conall waved around her clinic. "You handled all the current patients, and you mentioned how Liza will handle the rest, so you're good to go for a holiday, right?" She nodded and walked closer. He wrapped his arms around her and kissed her.

"I didn't expect to find you here," Bethany whispered.

"I didn't expect to find you here either," Conall admitted, tilting her head back and kissing her on the lips. "Now let's finish packing for our trip."

With him driving, they headed back to her apartment,

quickly double-checked their bags again, then loaded up and drove to the airport. It was a bit of a drive, but they got there in plenty of time.

Arriving in Hawaii many hours later, they made their way to the hotel. She stretched out on the bed and muttered, "You know something? For the first time in what seems like many years, I feel like maybe I can grab some sleep. Like, a lot of sleep."

"Then sleep," he said, as he tucked their bags off to the side. "We can unpack later, and we can also go for a swim whenever you want."

But she was already shifting onto her side. "I just need to crash."

He smiled. "I won't say no to napping with you." He dropped on the bed beside her, pulled her into his arms, and the two of them napped. He woke a little later to see that she had shifted and was staring up at him.

"You know something," she began, "there's being a gentleman, then there's being a gentleman."

His eyebrows rose. "What the hell does that mean?"

"It means, you're being too much of a gentleman."

"And more specifically that means?"

She smiled, then kissed him. "It means that we could move this along a little faster. Like a lot faster."

"Ah, so being a gentleman in that way."

"Yes," she muttered.

"Okay then." He tilted her slowly to her back. "I am totally okay with moving this forward."

"Good." She studied him closely. "When I said I wanted a holiday in Hawaii, … I meant a holiday in a whole bigger way."

"Interesting." He chuckled. "Exactly what do you have

in mind?"

She wrapped her arms around him and opened her thighs wide, settling him right where she wanted him. Now wrapping her legs around his hips, she pulled him close, then whispered, "A whole lot of this."

He chuckled, as he shifted his hips against her. "If I'd realized …"

"Oh, you realized," she said. "You were just giving me time."

He nodded. "I was giving you time, but if you don't *need* time …"

"I've had time," she said, with a smile, "and I'm totally good to be here. As a matter of fact, I'm absolutely delighted."

"Me too."

"My mom wishes us both the best, and, as usual she's jumping the gun, wanting to know if we were serious."

"You mean, as in marriage and all that good stuff?"

"Yeah, I'm pretty sure that's what she was hinting at."

"And this is from the same woman who was secretly living with Joe but maintaining two residences, trying not to let anybody know?"

"Yeah, and that's why she wants to know if we're serious," Bethany explained. "She spent a lot of time trying to hide her relationship and eventually not giving a damn, knowing Joe would never move in with her until she married him."

"Maybe they'll get married now."

"I hope so. They've been together a very long time."

"We know that they love each other," Conall said, "so let them live their lives fully now."

"That's the plan," she whispered, as she shifted her hips

up and down against him. Grabbing his ears, she tugged him closer. "You are wearing way-too-many clothes."

He laughed. "I'm wearing the same amount as you are, but I'm happy to wear less, if you prefer."

Hopping off the bed, he quickly stripped down to nothing. He stood in front of her and then hesitated a bit. "You want the leg on or off?"

Her eyes opened wide, as she stared at him. "You know something? That's damn sexy." She hopped to her knees, staring at the way the prosthetic met his leg. "Does it hurt?"

"No, not at all, but I also don't want you to hide from it or to think I'll hide it."

"God no." She ran her fingers up and down the steel. "I really like it." She grinned at him. "It's definitely sexy."

He stared at her in surprise and started to laugh. "Somehow I don't think very many women in the world would agree with you."

"Oh, I think you're misjudging women," she said, with a grin, as she tore off her clothes just as quickly as he had. "I think you're completely underestimating women and what we like," she added, "and what we like is confident and capable men." With a big smile, she moved closer. "Men who we know will protect us, even though we want to protect ourselves. Don't get me wrong. I'm all about looking after myself, but definitely something is special about knowing that a man will be there to back me up, if ever I need to fall."

"And if you ever need to fall," he added, "if nothing else, I can fall first and make for a softer landing."

She looked at him, and tears came to her eyes. "I really want to giggle at your words, but that image is so important. I also know that you mean it, and that is so important too. I am so looking forward to this holiday and the time we'll have together."

"Me too," he admitted. "It feels like forever since I had time to myself, time for anyone else," he muttered, as he took her in his arms, while she still kneeled on the bed. "Now it's time for the two of us, and we deserve it."

"We sure do," she whispered. She kissed him, but that kiss quickly turned to a kiss of power and passion, as both of them became overwhelmed with the joy of the freedom to be themselves, of the freedom they had to be here together, just the two of them with time to explore and to get to know each other.

By the time the kiss had to stop so they could breathe again, they collapsed back down on the bed. She was trembling, a complete wreck. She whispered, "God, if we'd realized …"

"I know," he whispered back. "I would have taken you to bed a long time ago."

She chuckled. "You did know already, didn't you?"

"I was hoping," he whispered, "but I didn't want to rush you. I wanted you coming to me, knowing full well who and what I was and what I had to offer."

She opened her arms, as he settled between her thighs and whispered, "It's all about who you really are, under that big scary facade, and you are 100 percent heart."

Quickly passion overwhelmed the two of them, as they raced to a goal of mutual satisfaction and joy. When he withdrew a little later and pulled her into his arms, he held her close and whispered, "The thought of getting dressed and going down to the pool or getting even more dressed and going out for dinner really doesn't appeal to me at all right now."

She rolled over, half on his chest, and gave him a lazy smile. "Do you know what does appeal?" When he raised an eyebrow, she nodded and added, "Room service and as much time alone together as we want." She lowered her head and kissed him. "Personally, I would be okay to spend the next fourteen days right here. Although there will be statements to give and questions to answer somewhere in there."

He laughed with delight, then flipped her to her back and nodded. "I'm not against that, as long as we come up for air once in a while."

"Later," she whispered, as she pulled his head down and kissed him with a deep, searing kiss. "Much later."

# EPILOGUE

B ADGER LOOKED OVER at Kat. "Aren't you tricky?"

She shrugged. "Not necessarily," she said, with a smile, "but it worked out for Bacchus and Michael and Danny and Mariam, plus Conall and Bethany, even her mom and Old Joe. So *three* happy families, and, for that, I'm very happy."

"Now what?" he asked, as he looked at the two files on her desk. "Who are you thinking for the next miracle?"

"I'm not so sure. … This one's a bit trickier."

"Why is that?"

"A hurricane in Florida," she murmured. "The War Dog was on the road with other dogs being transported out of the area. The truck ended up in the river. Details are sketchy, and I might not have this completely right, but it sounds like the driver, who may have been the transport truck owner, died. Several of the dogs managed to get free and were captured again, but the War Dog is missing."

He stared at her. "A hurricane? Were they in the back of the truck in cages or what?"

"Most were in cages, and some of them were still fine when the truck was found in the river. The cage the War Dog had been in was open, and he is still missing. Several other cages were also open, and those dogs were picked up again, but not the War Dog."

"Where were they taken to?"

"I don't know. As I said, the details are unclear. One guy was airlifted out. I assume he was in the passenger seat of the transport truck. He died too? Although I'm not certain. The animals were gathered up by a rescue team and were moved to a safe location," she shared. "And, of the missing animals, … we don't know any more."

Badger shook his head. "A hurricane."

She nodded. "Yeah, and it happened recently, so there's a good chance the War Dog is okay, and they have a lot of survival skills. Thus we have a good chance of recovering this one. I do have somebody in mind but—"

"What's with the *but?*"

She winced. "His brother died in the vehicle."

Badger let out a long whistle. "You're talking about Baron, aren't you?"

She nodded. "I don't know if it's fair to ask him to go after the dog that his brother was trying to rescue."

"On the other hand," Badger pointed out, "better that it wasn't in vain."

She smiled, then nodded. "I was thinking of that as well. I texted him earlier, but I haven't heard back yet."

Her phone rang just then. She looked down and raised one eyebrow. "Speaking of …"

He nodded, anxious to hear how Baron was doing. Kat punched the button to answer.

Baron's tired voice came through on the other end. "Kat, what's up?"

"Hey, I'm so sorry to hear about your brother."

"Yeah, me too. It's just too awful to imagine."

"Look. I don't know if you heard anything about some of the work we've been doing—"

"Yeah, War Dogs," he interrupted. "My brother was rescuing one."

"Right, and that's one of the reasons I called. I was wondering if you would want to give us a hand."

"What's up?"

"One War Dog is still missing."

"I know. It was in my brother's truck, but I haven't seen or heard anything else about it."

"I guess what I'm asking is, could you track it down?"

"*Right.* That's what you do, isn't it?"

"Yes, we track down War Dogs, but it sounds as if maybe your brother had this dog for a while."

"Actually he didn't. He was away for surgery and subsequent rehab. So somebody else was looking after the dog. When he got back home again, the War Dog didn't get returned."

"How did this one end up in your brother's truck then?"

"I don't think we have any paperwork, since everything happened in such a panic with the hurricane," he explained, his voice tired. "Everybody is saying that dog was in the back of the transport, but I don't know if that's really true. Are you sure you want *me* to track down this War Dog?"

"That's what we do," she said. "We find volunteers to get boots on the ground. I realize it's an odd request, since you've just lost your brother, and the area is in such turmoil, and everybody is trying to recover."

"We've got all the people accounted for, but we've got so much clean-up and rebuilding to do to get families housed and businesses restored. On a personal note, I just buried my brother," he added. "Yet you're right. A couple other dogs are still missing, and thankfully they didn't die with my brother. By the way, his death wasn't because of the hurricane itself. Not directly anyway. He'd always had a weak heart valve, and we knew it could fail at any time. He ended up having a heart attack in the process, and that's why he drowned. It wasn't really the hurricane or even the rescuing of the animals." He took a moment and collected his thoughts. "Any dog that needs a hand, well, I'm just as bad as my brother."

"How's your new foot?"

He laughed. "As always, you were right on target. It's doing better, and I'm becoming more capable with it."

"Good," she replied warmly.

"Okay, fine. I'm game," he said. "Give me a few days to see what I can come up with."

"That sounds good, and again, my condolences to you and your family."

"Thank you," he murmured. "Nothing quite like that kind of a loss, but I don't want it to be in vain. He was out helping animals, so I can go help the same animals and make sure the work he was doing gets completed." Baron sighed. "I'll see what I can come up with." And, with that, he rang off.

Badger looked over at her, one eyebrow raised. "At least he's right there in the area."

"He is, but what happened to the War Dog in the first place sounds a little sketchy to me."

"That seems to be why these cases end up on our desks," he noted, with a tilt of his head. "I don't suppose a ladylove or anything is in Baron's background, is there?"

Kat shrugged and gave him a knowing smile.

Badger narrowed his gaze.

"He did tell me one time that his brother's former wife was first Baron's girlfriend for the longest time. Apparently they broke up at some point, and she hooked up with his brother and married him very quickly afterward. It created a lot of trouble in the family for a long time, including separating the brothers."

"Something like that would surely do it," Badger noted.

"She contacted Baron a while back, and he wouldn't have anything to do with her."

Badger chuckled. "That doesn't mean Baron wants to have anything to do with her now either."

"No, but he might, considering that she tossed off Baron's child as his brother's."

"Oh, ouch."

She nodded.

"And you really think he'll want anything to do with her after all that?"

"It depends on what her reasoning was," Kat suggested. "Who are we to judge? We've all done stupid things in our lives."

He nodded. "Isn't that the truth," he muttered. He walked over, pulled her to her feet, and gave her a big hug. "I do love you. You know that, right?"

"I know you do," she murmured, "and that's a really smart answer right now."

He chuckled, held her close. "You are also incredibly amazing, and I'm so very proud to have you as my partner in this life."

"Ditto," she said, as she pulled him down, gave him a tongue-lashing kiss that had his head swimming. "Now we need to take a break and go for a swim, spend time together."

And, with that, she turned and walked out back to the pool, leaving him watching in awe, as this woman of his joined the other men who made up the Titanium Corp and their partners, making Badger's world complete.

This concludes Book 24 of The K9 Files: Conall.

Read about Baron: The K9 Files, Book 25

# The K9 Files: Baron (Book #25)

Welcome to the all new K9 Files series reconnecting readers with the unforgettable men from SEALs of Steel in a new series of action packed, page turning romantic suspense that fans have come to expect from USA TODAY Bestselling author Dale Mayer. Pssst... you'll meet other favorite characters from SEALs of Honor and Heroes for Hire too!

The hurricane devastated more than just Baron's world. It hurt so many other people too, including Baron's brother, who died trying to rescue dogs caught up in the storm. One of the missing dogs is a War Dog, Kingston. Now Baron is put on the spot to see if he could find the War Dog again …

Brittany's grandmother's house was destroyed in the hurricane, so Brittany has been searching for her grandmother's little dog, Pocket. When Baron comes to her aid, Brittany remembers her grandmother's warnings about those who take advantage during disasters …

During the aftermath of the hurricane, these two people are looking for missing animals, yet are about to get caught up in the middle of something no one saw coming …

Find Book 25 here!
To find out more visit Dale Mayer's website.
https://geni.us/DMSBaron

# Author's Note

Thank you for reading Conall: The K9 Files, Book 24! If you enjoyed the book, please take a moment and leave a short review.

Dear reader,

I love to hear from readers, and you can contact me at my website: www.dalemayer.com or at my Facebook author page. To be informed of new releases and special offers, sign up for my newsletter or follow me on BookBub. And if you are interested in joining Dale Mayer's Reader Group, here is the Facebook sign up page.
http://geni.us/DaleMayerFBGroup

Cheers,
Dale Mayer

# About the Author

Dale Mayer is a *USA Today* best-selling author, best known for her SEALs military romances, her Psychic Visions series, and her Lovely Lethal Garden cozy series. Her contemporary romances are raw and full of passion and emotion (Broken But … Mending, Hathaway House series). Her thrillers will keep you guessing (Kate Morgan, By Death series), and her romantic comedies will keep you giggling (*It's a Dog's Life*, a stand-alone novella; and the Broken Protocols series, starring Charming Marvin, the cat).

Dale honors the stories that come to her—and some of them are crazy, break all the rules and cross multiple genres!

To go with her fiction, she also writes nonfiction in many different fields, with books available on résumé writing, companion gardening, and the US mortgage system. All her books are available in print and ebook format.

## Connect with Dale Mayer Online

*Dale's Website – www.dalemayer.com*
*Twitter – @DaleMayer*
*Facebook Page – geni.us/DaleMayerFBFanPage*
*Facebook Group – geni.us/DaleMayerFBGroup*
*BookBub – geni.us/DaleMayerBookbub*
*Instagram – geni.us/DaleMayerInstagram*
*Goodreads – geni.us/DaleMayerGoodreads*
*Newsletter – geni.us/DaleNews*